AN UNTRUTHFUL DECLARATION

SIMON HARE

Published in 2009 by New Generation Publishing

First Edition

Chapter 1

According to my doctor, the psychiatrist had mentioned something about outbursts of uncontrollable anger, depression, sexual fantasies, alienation and detachment, obsessive behaviour and paranoia. I wasn't really interested in his problems though, I'd got enough of my own. The fact is I was being followed. My life was in danger. Someone was trying to kill me. I told him this, but he just fingered the little pubic beard that sprouted off his chin and shrugged it off. It started three days ago when I went out for a packet of cigarettes and a newspaper. I'd only walked about fifty yards when I heard footsteps behind me and realized what was happening. When I stopped, he stopped. When I came out of Patel's corner shop he was there outside looking up at the sky waiting for me to come out. He followed me back to Albion Mansions. I could hear his heavy footsteps behind me. He drives an old Ford Cortina; a green one; the side of its badly dented. He's been parking it at odd times directly outside the building; he just sits in it and keeps staring up at my room. He's there now, in the driver's seat pretending to read a newspaper. Paranoid my arse. Mr Sigmund bloody Freud ought to take a look out of the window now; he could see for himself.

Well that's it; I've had enough, I'll go down and ask him what the bloody hell's he playing at? I'm not putting up with this. He'd better come clean and tell me what this is all about or else. No one plays games with me.

I carefully drew the flimsy net curtain back a couple of inches and peeked out. There through the sea mist I could see sitting him in his car; a large fellow in a dark overcoat wearing gold half moon glasses pretending to read a newspaper. At that precise moment he must have sensed that I was looking at him. He gave a furtive glance up towards the top of the building and quickly looked down again before unfolding a further section of his newspaper.

'Right that's it', I said to myself and ran down the ten flights of stairs to the ground floor walked over to the car and tapped on the window.

"Excuse me," I said in a strained falsetto voice.

"Yes," he replied, as he begrudgingly wound down the window.

"I'm sorry to bother you," I said. "I'm wondering if I might be of any assistance."

"Come again," he said.

"I live in that building opposite and I couldn't help noticing that you seem to be looking for someone. If I can help in any way . . . my name is Tom Dunford."

"Thank you, but I'm not looking for anyone," he replied.

"Oh right, sorry to have troubled you."

"No trouble," he said, and wound up the window.

Feeling angry and frustrated at my blatant failure to assert myself, I slowly walked back and hovered inside the entrance of the building. 'Fool! . . . Bloody fool'. I said to myself scathingly. That was completely pointless. Now go back and ask him directly; why is he watching me? Why is he following me? Ask him directly

. . . come straight out with it . . . Confront him for Christ's sake. . . Confront the situation.

After a few minutes I regained my composure. I gave myself a stern reprimand for being so ineffectual and headed towards the car again. My approach was much the same.

"Excuse me," I said, this time in a practiced deep macho voice.

He wound the window down about half way and stared at me dispassionately.

"Look, I've tried to be polite but to no avail. I want to know why you are watching me. . . Why are you are following me?"

"You're mistaken," he said, turned the key in the ignition, and slowly drove away. I stood there for a few moments feeling utterly perplexed.

It was now seven fifteen. I climbed the stairs back up to my room, sat on the bed and lighted a cigarette. The room was bitterly cold and stank of failure. A loose pane of glass was vibrating in the old sash window from the bus exhausts outside. I stubbed the half smoked cigarette out in the eye of a grinning plaster Pekinese dog that sat on the mantelpiece and headed off to the bathroom I shared with four other residents. If I didn't commandeer it now and beat them to it, the water would be freezing cold. Not only that, Eric: Eric Bottomly had some pretty nasty habits which I won't go into; suffice it to say that he'd evolved from some specie of marine reptile. No one, believe me, would want to use anything after him.

The face that peered back at me in the bathroom mirror wasn't mine. It was old, haunted: I sighed gently, resigned to the fact that it was ageing rapidly. The wispy grey hair on top of it was receding at an alarming rate. The soulless pale blue eyes with dark grey bags under them accentuated its unhealthy countenance. When I did find the courage to face up to it I would mournfully reflect that this face was the product of thirty two years and five months of utter waste and disillusionment. It hadn't achieved anything remotely worth recounting. The few brief relationships it'd had with women were wishy-washy affairs that invariably came to nothing. According to Julia; its last girl friend, it was afraid of commitment. Mind you, if you knew her, you might understand why.

It was seven thirty when I returned from the bathroom with my hair still dripping wet. I paced up and down the room for another ten minutes; smoked three more cigarettes, released a consumptive wheeze and realized I'd better get myself down to the dining room. In another five minutes Mrs Hoskins would be flapping around and getting herself in a state over the breakfast routine. The deal I'd struck with her: the room, breakfast, and an evening meal for seventy five pounds a week, was good value and nowadays becoming increasingly harder to find.

Six months ago I'd made the boldest move in my life. I resigned from the insurance company I'd been with since I left school in order to fulfil a life long ambition of becoming a writer. I'd saved just enough money to live modestly for a year in the hope that it would give me enough time to establish a new career. Being naïve and deluded, the few minor successes I'd had offered some encouragement; a couple of short stories published and half a dozen articles for some glossy magazines. The challenge now was to write a novel. Not just any old novel, but a best seller; a murder mystery cliff hanger that would sell in the millions. Oh yes, all the major players would be gagging to get hold of it. Okay, the progression towards this goal couldn't exactly be described as rapid, although it did seem to be taking shape. Nearly half of it was completed and 'reading well' according to the few hapless friends I had who'd volunteered to proffer opinions.

Now, and for the past three days, my writing had come to a standstill. I couldn't concentrate, my anxiety level was reaching fever pitch. This couldn't go on.

When I first viewed the 'serviced apartments' that were advertised four months ago, I was immediately taken with Albion Mansions. The faded decadent charm of the Victorian apartment block situated just off the seafront in Brighton, offered great nostalgic appeal. The building, the homely Mrs Hoskins, and particularly the dining room, were all so reminiscent of the seaside boarding houses that I'd stayed at as a child. Those unforgettable days of endless summer sunshine: sand castles, fish and chips, candy floss and . . . the pier. Oh yes! Those magical holidays spent with my parents in the nineteen fifties would always remain etched in my memory. The first one I remember was in the year of the coronation when I was only five in Shanklin on the Isle of Wight. It was on the beach during that particular holiday that I made the biggest discovery in my life. I learned that girls were not *exactly* the same as boys.

The only minor drawback here was that meals were served in the dingy basement dining room. Descending the twelve flights of stairs from my attic room didn't seem to present that much of a problem: however, I failed to consider the difficulties presented in climbing them again with acute dyspepsia after one of Mrs Hoskins ample portions of Irish stew, and more often than not, one of her generous servings of home made apple pie. The last thing I wanted to do was seem ungrateful despite the rigid time schedules laid down that were so vitally important to her.

Now hopelessly defeated, I made my way into the dining room. All the tables were taken up with other residents who were 'half boarders' as Mrs Hoskins called them. There were only six including me. A few nods and grunts were forthcoming as I walked past them towards *my* table; even more niggled now at my ineptitude in resolving the situation. This morning, because of the disruption in my normal routine, I'd neglected to buy a newspaper. This immediately put me into a foul mood. How could I possibly sit here and eat breakfast without something to read?

The epicurean delights of breakfast did little to lift my spirits. From Monday to Friday the exotic fare provided by Mrs Hoskins was a bowl of economy no nonsense cereal, followed by toast and marmalade, and two cups of incredibly weak tea. On Saturdays and Sundays, it was possible to indulge in a full English breakfast for an additional five pounds a week. In an effort to conserve my meagre funds I had so far resisted this temptation. My stoic efforts to shun this extravagance were though seriously tested as the delicious aroma of bacon permeated all twelve flights of stairs up to my room.

Being shy and overly sensitive, I'd failed to get to know any of the other residents. There were two that had spoken to me a couple of times. One of them was Roy Benson; a stocky affable character who was evidently a self employed insurance salesman. Apparently his world collapsed five years ago when his 'cow' of a wife found a younger replacement. He'd lost his house, his business, and everything else he owned through the divorce, and ended up going bankrupt paying legal fees. He said he wasn't bitter about it now, which just meant he was either a liar or mentally ill. He'd been living at 'The Mansions' as he called them for nearly five years now and confidently confirmed that he was 'picking up the threads', whatever the hell that was supposed to mean.

My other brief encounter was with Eric Bottomly. I mentioned before; there really was something very strange about Eric. Nature had certainly not been kind to him. In certain lights he bore a close resemblance to a prehistoric sea turtle with his pointed face and slanted reptilian eyes. I suspected . . . well, not just suspected, I knew this man was up to all kinds of dreadful things. Sometimes I would lie awake at night with my fertile imagination running riot thinking about the gruesome activities Eric was undoubtedly indulging in.

I was now becoming increasingly irritated by the lack of anything to read. At least this might have taken my mind off things, if only for half an hour or so. This evil swine that was following me had now succeeded in upsetting my equilibrium. Not just preventing me from writing; but now interfering with my breakfast. I slowly got up from the table before the toast buttering ritual commenced, walked out of the dining room, ran up the flight of stairs to the ground floor and headed towards the front of the building. I opened the main front door very slowly hoping to prevent the wretched brass bell from ringing that was attached to it. The last thing I needed was Mrs Hoskins running up after me wanting to know why I'd left my breakfast. An attempted casual look up and down the road confirmed my worse fears: the old Cortina had returned. Inside, the same man was staring up at my window, this time . . . through a small pair of binoculars.

With my heart racing I ran off in the opposite direction to Patel's corner shop; bought a newspaper and a packet of cigarettes and ran back. As I opened the front door, the bloody bell which I'd quite forgotten about, clanged loudly causing Mrs Hosking to totter up from the dining room to see who it was. She stood in front of me blocking my return down the flight of stairs to the dining room.

"Oh it's you Mr Dunford, is everything alright?" she asked breathlessly, whilst drying her hands on her apron.

"Yes, everything's fine, well, that's not exactly true . . . I think somebody's trying to kill me. Perhaps I might have a word with you after breakfast if that would be alright?"

"Why yes of course dear," she said. "Now you go and finish your breakfast before your toast gets cold. Nothing worse than cold toast, that's what I always think."

I realized Mrs Hoskins was just being maternal. She didn't want me to meet my maker on an empty stomach.

When I returned to the dining room the other 'half boarders' had left. I propped my newspaper up behind a jar of 'economy blend' marmalade and proceeded to devour the cold and now brittle toast. Mrs Hoskins was scurrying about in the kitchen washing up the breakfast things and humming some loathsome tune. I waited another ten minutes then strolled over nervously to where she was.

"Excuse me Mrs Hoskins, would this ɔe a convenient time to have a word?"

"Yes of course dear, what's the problem?"

"Well, this might sound strange to you, but I am wondering if anyone has been here asking questions about me?"

Mrs Hoskins looked perplexed by this and conducted an in depth study of my face before answering.

"No. Why do you ask dear?"

"Well this probably sounds ridiculous, but for the past three days somebody has been following me. Every time I leave the building . . . a man . . . this particular man follows me. He's there *now* outside, sitting in his car. I think he must be a hired assassin.

"Following you?" she repeated, still completely ignoring the fact that I'd only got a short while to live. "Why would he be following you dear?"

"I don't know why . . . I can't think of a reason, but he *is* believe me."

"Oh I'm sure your right dear, perhaps he's a private detective, that's the sort of thing they do dear. I know Jack and I saw a lovely old film the other night: this private detective was watching somebody just as you've described. Oh it was a lovely film; they don't make them like that any more."

"Yes, I'm sure it was," I said. "The thing is I think my life is in danger."

"Now look, don't take this the wrong way dear, but you haven't been over doing it what with all this writing you're doing have you? I remember you told me when you took the room you were trying to write a murder mystery novel. You know you wanted a quiet room so that's why I put you at the top."

"No, I appreciate that Mrs Hoskins. It was very considerate of you to think of this. There's nothing wrong with the room. It's quiet, in fact it's perfect. I am very happy here that's not the problem. I just . . ."

"Why don't you go to the police?"

"Well to be honest if I did that, I suspect the police would think I was having some sort of nervous breakdown . . . becoming paranoid."

"Oh I don't know dear, they can be very helpful. I know when we lost Arthur a few years ago they were so helpful, and I must say they couldn't really have done more for us."

"I'm sorry, who was Arthur?"

"Arthur was our cat dear. We'd had him for ten years, and all of a sudden he just disappeared. They never actually found him, but I know they did everything they possibly could. If you're worried I should go to them dear."

"Look Mrs Hoskins, I know this might sound strange to you, but would you please come with me to the front of the house and I'll point him out to you. I know you've lived here for a long time; you might even know who it is."

"Alright dear, just let me put the dishes in the sink and find my coat only it's bitterly cold out there. You go on up, and I'll see you in the hall upstairs in a couple of minutes."

"Thank you Mrs Hoskins this really is very kind of you. I'm so sorry to be a nuisance I do realise you're busy."

A few minutes later she appeared as if prepared for an Arctic expedition.

"Right; now dear, let's go outside and you point him out to me. I don't see why we shouldn't go over and ask him what he wants," she said comfortingly as if placating a child.

We both looked up and down the road. Not a trace was to be seen of the man in the car. Despite the fact that it was now raining steadily with a raw easterly wind blowing in gusts, Mrs Hoskins insisted that we walk up and down to each end of the road to see if he had parked up somewhere.

"Oh well," she said, as we went back into the house soaked to the skin, "if you see him again, and you're worried, you tell me straight away, alright dear?"

"Yes, yes," I agreed, feeling terribly guilty for dragging her out of her warm kitchen and realizing now that she simply didn't believe me. I had a sudden flashback to my childhood. At seven years of age I suffered night terror fits imagining 'something' was in my room. After hours of hysterical screaming and crying I would finally be coaxed back to bed after my mother assured me there was no one there.   Why did I mention it to Mrs Hoskins in the first place? Surely I should have guessed that anything like this was beyond her sphere of comprehension. The fact that I'd confided in her; a pleasant, but nonetheless silly old woman, was an ominous manifestation of my increasing desperation. Was this whole thing part of an evil plan to push me over the edge? But by whom? Who would be perverse enough to do this to me? Maybe I was just overreacting.

Soaking wet, and experiencing an overwhelming feeling of inertia, I stood in the hallway trying to gather my thoughts. One thing was certain: I mustn't let this situation interfere with my plan. If the book wasn't completed, everything would be of no consequence. I'd given up a good job; a promising career to live this penurious lifestyle for one reason, and for one reason only. No one now was going to stop me. The reasons for the strange behaviour of my persecutor may never be discovered, but this must be put to one side. Feeling slightly more positive after this considered assessment; I decided to walk into town and buy a few essentials that I'd been putting off. I needed a new typewriter ribbon, some more paper, stamps and envelopes.

The fine spitting rain had eased a little, but forceful gusts of bitterly cold wind drove straight through me occasioning a torrent of venomous expletives. Stopping to cross the road, I looked left, looked right and looked left again. I started; I could see from the corner of my eye, twenty yards behind was the man who'd been following me; now staring straight at me. Panicking, without thinking I ran straight into the traffic. Car horns blared; tyres screeched on the wet road and angry drivers shouted obscenities. Shoppers and passers by stopped dead in their tracks. I waved a hand up at the motorists apologetically running as fast as I could, knocking and bumping into people in my panic. After a couple of minutes I stopped . . . quite breathless holding my side. Looking back I glimpsed the man also running, clouds of steam billowing from his overworked lungs. Feeling exhausted and out of condition; I couldn't run any further. Leaning on a railing at the side of the road I tried to get my breath, transfixed on the figure walking slowly towards me. Realizing I'd now seen him, he stopped. He was standing by the kerb, watching the traffic as if to cross the road, at the same time keeping a close eye on me. He crossed over and walked quickly in my direction but on the other side of the road. After a couple of minutes he drew level with me, stopped again and lighted a cigarette. I couldn't contain my anguish any longer. I stood at the kerbside and shouted manically across the road. "I'm only going to 'Smith's' to buy a ribbon and some paper. You can come with me if you must!" Many people slowed down, stared at me assuming I was arguing with someone. They couldn't see who I was shouting at; and were instinctively waiting for a response. The man just stood there examining his fingernails with the cigarette in his mouth. I didn't care what anyone thought, I was feeling desperate. Just at that moment a taxi stopped briefly in the flow of traffic. Without thinking I opened the passenger door and jumped in next to the driver. "Please for Christ's sake . . . drive . . . drive as fast as you can . . . away from here . . . anywhere. Please it's urgent I'll explain . . . but please . . . go as fast as you can."

The taxi driver was insouciant: "alright mate, don't worry. Had a bust up with the wife have you?"

I turned around as the car moved forward to see what the man was going to do. He was gone; no sign of him anywhere. 'Thank God for that', I said to myself.

"Where would you like me to drop you mate?"

"Oh I don't know, just drive along the seafront road for a mile or so if you would and then drop me off somewhere near the town centre."

"Yeah, alright, alright. Don't let it get to you me ole mate. These things blow over. I get it with her indoors all the time. Hormonal problems . . . that's their bleeding trouble. Haven't met one yet that doesn't suffer from it."

"No, that's true," I agreed, knowing it would have been pointless trying to explain that I was about to be murdered.

He must be a mind reader I thought as the taxi pulled up outside Smith's the stationers. Oh shit: I muttered to myself; why did I tell the bloody man where I was going? I expect he'll be inside the shop waiting for me. I paid the driver, got out of the taxi and walked cautiously towards the shop. A good look around reassured me. There was no sign of the man. If he'd wanted to continue following me he would certainly have been there by now.

Buying a new ribbon for my typewriter should have been a simple matter. All I needed to do was to take out the old one, give it to the shop assistant and they'd know which one it was. But in my disturbed state of mind, I'd forgotten to take out the old one and bring it with me. When somebody's trying to kill you, you tend to forget about things like this. "Bugger," I muttered, and spent the next ten minutes examining various boxes of ribbons trying to remember which one looked like mine. The trouble was they all did. Suddenly everything went black. I was being attacked by someone from behind. Two hands were pressed firmly over my eyes and my head was being pulled back. I yelled out: 'Help, help me'. This was it, my time had come; he'd got here before me, I was being murdered in broad daylight, in a crowded shop. A woman let out a raucous husky laugh. I turned around and saw Julia creasing up with laughter.

"Goodness, you're nervous."

"Julia, for Christ's sake what's the matter with you? What a bloody stupid thing to do, I could have had a heart attack."

"Good God," she said, realizing now that she'd terrified the life out of me, "why are you so jumpy? You never used to be like that. Guilty conscience is it?"

"Oh I'm sorry Julia; it really *is* nice to see you. It's just . . . it's just my nerves are shot to pieces at the moment. Something strange is going on; I think somebody is after me. I know it probably sounds quite ridiculous, but there's this man . . ."

"Just as I thought," she said, displaying her infectious smile and even white teeth,   "you've finally gone mad. I knew it would happen sooner or later."

"No, I'm deadly serious, I . . ."

"What are you doing in here anyway?"

"A ribbon: I want a new ribbon for my typewriter but I forgot to take out the old one and now I'm . . ."

"Oh you are a Silly Billy," she said, interrupting me again and simultaneously poking me in the chest which was definitely one of her more infuriating habits. "Have you still got that old Olympia, that old manual contraption?"

"Yes, only it's not an old contraption, it's a finely engineered machine."

"No it's not, it's an old dinosaur, but anyway this is the one you need," she said, picking one of the shelf. "I'm surprised they still make them for antiques like that."

"Ah that's great, I just need to pick up some paper and envelopes and that's the shopping in here done for now. What are you up to anyway? What are you doing in here?"

"Oh it's my mother's birthday on Wednesday; I just popped in to buy her a card. It's my lunch hour. Some of us still need to work you know." Do you fancy joining me for a sandwich or something? I've still got three quarters of an hour. You can tell me all about this mysterious man who's following you."

I didn't need much persuading. Despite the bitter arguments that were an unpleasant feature in the last few days of our relationship; I was still fond of her. It would also nice to have some feminine company if only for half an hour or so.

Why did women have to be so bloody difficult? It always starts off alright; all laughter and joy . . . until they get their painted claws into you. They know exactly what they want but they don't let on until they've got you hooked. Masters at subterfuge! I thought to myself. I was feeling confused and resentful as we walked towards 'The Copper Kettle' tea rooms; a place I loathed with a vengeance; a fine example of sickening genteel

18

pretentiousness. It had been Julia's idea to go there. I knew it would have been pointless me suggesting the pub on the corner for example; which would have had a more congenial atmosphere. A stiff drink would have calmed my nerves a bit as well. Had she been less manipulative and dogmatic, we would probably still be together. Yes . . . it was all her fault. There was no doubt about it.

The first thing that hit me as we stepped inside was the vile smell: a heady mixture of moth balls, wet mackintoshes and gas effluvia emanating from the kitchen. The atmosphere was not that dissimilar to the service at a cremation I once attended. Most of the reproduction 'Jacobean' tables with their wheel back chairs were occupied by people well into retirement. Everyone in there spoke in frightened whispers; terrified not to cause offence by their presence. Oh what an odious place this was!

The young spotty faced waitress was horrified when Julia ordered a pot of tea for two and two portions of Welsh rarebit.

"I think we're only serving lunches at the moment," she said condescendingly, "but I'll check with the kitchen and see if that's possible."

Whoever was in the kitchen magnanimously acquiesced to this preposterous breach of the rules; much to my disappointment. I was still hoping that our audacious request would be denied, and we could then go to the pub after all.

"Now tell me seriously; what's all this nonsense about someone following you? You look absolutely dreadful."

Julia was not in the least bit inhibited by the church like quietness inside the tea rooms. Her effervescent personality made no provision for her voice to be lowered a few octaves, which would have been appropriate. Several old wizened faces craned their necks to get a good look at me. Understandably, they wanted to see what a man who was being followed actually looked like.

"Shush, it's difficult to talk in here, can't you see they're all listening."

"Bugger them," Julia said, letting out her husky semi bronchial laugh. "Might cheer them up . . . a nice bit of drama eh?   If they had something to talk about themselves they wouldn't be listening to us."

The room was now even quieter than before. People close to us all seemed to be preoccupied carrying out a close examination of both the floor and parts of the ceiling.

"It's not nonsense; it's true."

"What does he look like then?"

"Well, he's about fifty, maybe a bit older, about six foot and fairly well built. He wears a black Crombie overcoat, and gold coloured half moon glasses."

"He sounds really nice. Perhaps you ought to introduce him to me."

"Oh for Christ's sake Julia, this isn't a joke. Can't you take anything seriously?"

"Oh don't be so touchy. I can understand it must be worrying for you, but you seem to have lost your sense of humour. He *must be* a private detective. I expect he's got you mixed up with somebody else. These people do a lot of divorce cases. Perhaps if you told him who you are, he'd realize he'd got the wrong person."

"Well that's *precisely* what I did. I told him my name, I told him where I lived, and asked him why he was following me. He just said I must be mistaken. Mistaken! For Christ's sake. A few minutes later he's staring up at my room through a pair of binoculars. He even followed me here. I was only able to shake him off by jumping in a taxi and telling the driver to get away as fast as he could."

"Golly you *are* in a state. I'd go to the police if I were you. Perhaps he's some sort of mental case. On the other hand, just supposing he is a private detective: it could be that his client's wife is having a fling with somebody that fits your description, or lives in the same building you're in. He's not to know if it's you . . . is he? Unless . . . unless of course you're not telling me something."

"Oh Julia don't be so bloody ridiculous. If I was knocking off a married woman, I'd hardly be telling you about it. The other part of what you said though could possibly make sense . . . I suppose. If somebody has given him a description that fits mine; the fact that I've told him my name wouldn't necessarily make any difference. I could still be bedding his client's wife . . . Yes of course . . . that's almost certainly it. I now see why he was looking up from the road at my room through binoculars. He was hoping to see a scantily clad woman up there . . . God; he's not the only one! No doubt he's got a sophisticated camera in the car to take shots for the client. *That* would explain why he's been following me. That's it! He's expecting me to meet up with this mysterious woman somewhere. He can then take some incriminating photos and . . ."

"There you are you see, why do you do get yourself in such a state over nothing? There's always a simple explanation for everything."

Reluctantly I had to agree. I also had to agree that 'The Copper Kettle's Welsh rarebit was excellent. The earl grey tea wasn't that bad either.

Watching Julia hovering around the little desk waiting to pay the bill, I was contemplating what an attractive woman she was: slim, with long blonde hair, beautiful blue eyes, and unusually prominent cheek bones. Most men would have been overjoyed to find someone like her. Was she still on her own? I wondered. Although what difference could it possibly make? I suppose I liked to think that the option of reinstating our relationship was still there. Perhaps this might happen in a year's time when my book was published.

I'd known her for about four weeks before moving into her flat. Initially we were deliriously happy. However, it didn't take long for her dominant personality to come to the fore. She was four years younger than me. She'd wanted us to get married, buy a house, have children, and all the rest of it. I wasn't ready for this. It had all happened far too quickly. I could see my future mapped out by her, without being given a chance to consider what *I* wanted. The prospect of being stuck in the insurance company for a further thirty years, with a massive mortgage, and a couple of screaming babies was abhorrent. My plan to take a year out and write was undoubtedly hastened by this dangerously close brush with agonising conformity. It was of course the last straw for her . . . a disingenuous rejection. If I didn't want her on her terms, that was fine. There were plenty of men out there that would. She thought the idea of me quitting my job was ridiculous. According to her, we'd reached a point in our lives when we had everything to look forward to. I tried to explain that I wasn't looking forward to another thirty years with the insurance company but it was pointless. I was insane and should be sectioned for wanting to write. The arguments started, and they gathered momentum: I didn't really love her, I was just using her, I was too immature to have a proper relationship . . . and so it went on *ad infinitum*. A few weeks later my life was very different. No job, no girlfriend; the warm femininely sensual flat had been replaced with a cold seedy attic room on the fifth floor of Albion Mansions. Yes, there was no doubt in my mind. The writing just *had* to work.

Julia insisted that I must phone her if there were any interesting developments before she rushed back to work. I tried to interpret this to mean that she was still unattached.

Standing outside the restaurant in the biting wind I was overcome with soul wrenching melancholy. Why were everyone else's lives so straight forward? I was trying to gather my thoughts. Had I made a big mistake . . . misjudged the situation? How would I have felt if Julia had told me that she'd met the man of her dreams? No . . . I mustn't think like this, I was making myself feel worse. I didn't want her on her terms, yet I didn't want anyone else to have her either. This really was a perverse paradox. Why did she always have to dictate what *she* wanted all the time? Why couldn't she have been reasonable? Women!

As I stood there grimacing and shaking my head whilst conducting a brief but bitter analytical assessment of the position, people were beginning to stare at me. Realizing my presence outside the restaurant was now attracting attention; I forced myself to move on to the post office to buy some stamps.

My timing couldn't have been worse. It seemed the entire elderly population of the town had decided to draw their pensions out together. 'Bloody business' I muttered under my breath when after a fifteen minute wait, I finally got served.

Having concluded my business, I decided a brisk walk back might lift my spirits. The leaden sky was beginning to look threatening; the wind was getting up again; if I stepped on it I might just get back to Albion Mansions before receiving a further soaking.

Chapter 2

Whatever was going on in the room next to me certainly wasn't helping my concentration. I'd fitted the new ribbon and was intending to continue with my book. The thumps, bangs; the sound of voices, caused me to abandon a vital passage mid sentence. I stomped up and down in a furious temper, smoking and blowing out the smoke aggressively. What the hell was happening?

I sat down and tried once again to re-capture the crucial point where I'd left off, but it was futile. Being unable to contain myself any longer, I opened the door and saw Mrs Hoskins with Jack, her resident handyman, hauling an enormous mattress into the room. They seemed to have got it stuck and wedged in the doorway.

"Do you need a hand?" I asked, not really wanting to help; just really hoping for an apology, or at the very least, some sort of explanation.

"Oh hello dear," she said, "it's very kind of you but I think we can manage. I didn't think you were in, otherwise I would have knocked and had a word with you."

Jack: a taciturn ruddy faced character stared morosely at me from inside the room for a few seconds and then continued tugging at the mattress.

"There you are, I told you 'e' was probably in there;" he said, as if referring to a gerbil in a cage. "We could have saved ourselves all this trouble just by opening 'is' door a bit; we could 'ave' fed it this way a couple of feet," he said pointing to my room, "and it would 'ave' gone straight in; easy as pie."

"Don't worry," I said trying to conceal my contempt for this outrage. I leant over and pushed the top of the mattress for all I was worth; failing to take into account the fact that Jack was still tugging at it from the other side. All of a sudden it gave; went straight through the doorway and sprung open on the floor, like a giant rebellious monster with a life of its own. Jack was sent flying into the room and seemed to bounce twice on the floorboards.

"Bloody stupid idiot!" He shouted. "Why didn't you tell me you were pushing it? I wouldn't 'ave' pulled it so 'ard' from this side."

After fussing about and ensuring that Jack hadn't broken anything; Mrs Hoskins poked her head around the door and thanked me for my assistance.

"We're just getting the room ready for Mr Stubbs dear. He's a very nice man; I'm sure you and he will get on. I've told him that you're a writer, and you mustn't be disturbed and he's assured me that he'll be as quiet as a mouse."

"When's he moving in?" I asked, unable to disguise my trepidation.

"This evening dear. He said he can't wait to sample my toad in the hole ha-ha; he's going to be another 'half boarder' like you."

"What about the bathroom?" I asked, concerned that a change in the rota would mean I'd have to use the bath after Eric.

"Don't worry dear, nothing will change you can still have your bath every Friday night. It'll be Mr Stubbs's on

Thursday's, and nothing changes as far as the others are concerned."

"What does he do for a living?"

"Ah let me see, he did tell me . . . ah yes I think he said he's a photographer . . . yes that was it dear; a photographer. Had a bit of a sad life . . . apparently he lost his wife a few years ago and is still finding it hard to cope with. Right; we must get on now Mr Dunford; thank you very much for your help and I hope we didn't disturb you too much."

I nodded at her in a strange detached manner not wanting to reveal my true feelings, and retreated to my room. This really was outrageous. A complete betrayal. She'd emphatically told me that the room next to mine was only used for storage. As there were only two attic rooms, with mine being the only one occupied; my peace would be guaranteed. That's what she's said. . . Oh yes . . . that's definitely what she'd said when I first looked at the room. Up until now everything had been perfect. What was she playing at? Did she think she could go back on her word just like that? What a truly vile woman she was after all!

In absent minded thought I honed in on Jack. I'd spied him a number of times around the building always wearing the same vacuous expression. His tattered blue dungarees seemed to house an extraordinary collection of tools, with pliers and pincers being unquestionably his favourite; at least a dozen pairs of these hung from a wide leather belt that seemed to hold everything together. The most notable feature of Jack was his permanent disgruntled jowly rictus. If there were any truth in the theory of evolution, Jack certainly hasn't got very far as yet; he could well have been on this earth scores of times, but any progress in his development was painfully slow.

I paced up and down the room for another ten minutes cursing vehemently. After smoking three cigarettes which had left a foul taste in my mouth; I sat in front of the typewriter again hoping to recover some inspiration. The whole bloody day had nearly gone and all I'd produced were three pathetic lines. But at least now calm seemed to have been restored. I got up and carefully opened my door a few inches and listened. Yes . . . thank God; they'd gone. It was now four o'clock; I'd got another three hours; with any luck I'd be able to write half a dozen pages before savouring more of Mrs Hoskins' gastronomic delicacies.

A quick look out of the window made me feel a little easier. It was now beginning to get dark, the wind driven fine rain was hitting the window in persistent bursts. An empty plastic bag was floating around in the wind like a bird that had lost its direction; swooping up and down with celestial grace.   The street below was now almost deserted. There was no sign of the Ford Cortina or the man. Julia was almost certainly right. He *is* a private detective. As soon as he realizes that I'm not up to some nefarious activity with his client's wife he'll go and follow a different scent, stalking somebody else.

Whether by a stroke of luck or perhaps some divine intervention, my inspiration returned. I tapped away for two hours solidly. I'd written another six pages . . . and they were good! I read through it all again making a few minor corrections and congratulated myself on this magnificent effort in the face of such adversity. Then all of a sudden –Bang! - The lights went out. The room was pitch black. I carefully felt my way over to the window and peered out. None of the other lights in the road were out. It wasn't a power cut; it must just be a problem here. Creeping and feeling my way over to the door, I opened it and saw somebody crouching with a torch inside the cupboard on the landing; "Bloody main fuse 'as gorn' up 'ere'. I walked a little closer and recognised Jack from the display of pliers hanging from him.

"How long is it going to be?" I asked.

"As long as it bloody takes!" was the considered reply.

At the last minute, in an attempt to install a further power point for the new occupant; ham-fisted Jack had managed to completely disable the power supply to the top two floors. He must have been working very quietly next door, because I was quite oblivious to his presence. More than likely he had been cautioned by Mrs Hoskins that 'their young writer' mustn't be disturbed. An instruction of this nature wouldn't have boded well with somebody like Jack.

Jack was of the old school . . . nothing other than a good days work for a good days pay. He'd probably never read a book in his life. No doubt in his eyes, the people that wrote them, particularly if they were young and able bodied, were to be viewed with the utmost suspicion and contempt. What was wrong with them! Why couldn't they do a 'proper job' like everyone else!

The prospect of sitting in my blackened room for another hour until the toad in the hole appeared was not appealing. Nor was the option of sitting in the dingy dining room for this amount of time either. The best thing to do I decided, would be to go across the road to the Crown and Anchor and relax with a decent pint of real ale. If I took the six sheets I'd just written with me, I could re-read them again and revel in my own glory. I fumbled my way over to the typewriter picked up the last six sheets, stuffed them in my pocket and cautiously made my way down.

As I stepped outside the safety of Albion Mansions I was hit with an icy blast of wind and rain. The weather was definitely getting worse. The usual six o'clock rush hour traffic was building up making it a major effort simply to cross the road.

The warm friendly atmosphere though inside the saloon bar immediately lifted my spirits. The barmaid, who I'd never seen before was another attraction. A handful of regulars were sitting around with two of them propping up the bar. I ordered a pint of 'best' and retreated to a small table in the corner. Out came the last six pages which had been screwed up in my pocket. I straightened them out as best I could and the self aggrandisement continued. The first pint disappeared within minutes. My sense of buoyancy knew no bounds. I'd cracked it! The disposal of the body: the red herrings, the subterfuge, and the twist in the plot . . . this was excellent . . . *no agent* could turn this one down. No more rejection slips with the ubiquitous 'not for us' or 'not for our list' on them. This time they'd better take note! Sit up and listen! There: sitting right in front of them would be a best seller, a blockbuster with potential film rights and all the rest of it.

Ha-ha, at last, success and fame were staring me in the face. I got up and ordered another pint, even managing a little jocular bonhomie with the new barmaid: 'How could it be that I'd never seen her here before', and 'Oh, how her beautiful smile brightens the place up', etc. Some of the locals could clearly be seen cringing, undoubtedly amazed at what they thought was a toe curling pathetic little creep, trying it on with such an experienced buxom wench; obviously none of them realized that I was about to become a famous author. I drank the second pint standing at the bar, trying unsuccessfully to keep up this ebullient charade, but was now conscious of being observed. It was now nearing seven o'clock; I lifted my glass to swallow the last few dregs when Roy Benson slapped me on the back nearly knocking me over.

"Just spotted you from the public bar, we must have a quick one together, what do you say eh?"
Before I had a chance to decline his generous offer, the barmaid was instructed to 'go on, fill 'em'up again'.

"Cheers he bellowed," swallowing nearly half of his pint in one go. "Got to keep the old horse watered you know, ha-ha, we don't want anyone in here dying here from dehydration. Life's hard enough as it is ha-ha."

I wasn't used to drinking, or moreover; drinking this quickly. I drank as much of my third pint without breathing in as I could in a failed attempt to keep up. Finally I somehow managed by taking smaller sips, which enabled me to finish it shortly after him. I was now feeling full to bursting, but knew I'd have to return the compliment. I banged my pint glass down on the counter and instructed the barmaid to re-fill both our glasses.

"Not going back for dinner tonight then?" he said.

"Well, I had intended to, but it's a bit late now."

"Hmm, perhaps we ought to finish this one and get back over there. After all it's toad in the hole tonight. I don't know about you me old matey, but I always think that old mother Hoskins excels herself at that one. If we're only half an hour late; if it's cold, she might even put it back in the oven again for a few minutes for us."

Benson clearly had the drinking capacity of a camel. I was only half way through my pint by the time he'd finished his, and had now ordered a couple of large scotches 'for the road'. After three large slurps and an unseemly eructation, I banged my empty glass back on the bar. I didn't have time to object to the large whisky that was on the bar in front of me now, and was reluctant to offend him by leaving it. In a final act of bravado, I picked it up shouted in a slurred voice: 'bottoms up' and swallowed it in one. I wasn't feeling at all well now. I seemed to be sweating profusely; everything was half rotating around me. Strange cacophonies of sounds were whirling around in my head. I started feeling very sick. The mental image I conjured up of congealed toad in the hole increased the impending waves of nausea. Finding it difficult to control my now rubbery legs, I managed to drag myself outside, with Benson holding my arm whilst jabbering away facile platitudes, completely oblivious of my delicate condition. Suddenly both of us were covered in buff coloured vomit.

Back at Albion Mansions we avoided bumping into anyone. Benson helped me up to my room, and went off to change; still hoping to devour not only his dinner, but perhaps mine as well, given the unfortunate circumstances.

At five o'clock the next morning I woke up frozen to the marrow. I felt dreadful. My mouth was firmly stuck together; I was still fully clothed; the whole room stank of vomit and stale alcohol. The first attempt to lift my head off the pillow failed, when the dreadful thumping inside it heralded a grim reminder of last night's exuberance. I desperately needed to use the toilet but suspected that moving my head would result in a further vomiting attack. Yet another insoluble dilemma! The obvious solution I decided; was to get up extremely slowly, and apply a little self hypnosis. Being sick is for wimps I belatedly told myself. By incorporating this mind over matter strategy, and with a supreme mental effort, I eventually rose to my feet. Thirty seconds later the assumed efficacy of this proposition failed miserably as I wretched violently before reaching the door.

By eight o'clock although there was a slight improvement in my condition, I still couldn't face the prospect of breakfast. I managed to clean up the room and myself; and lay on my bed lamenting my foolishness, trying with great difficulty to analyze what could have promoted it.

At last I remembered. Yes . . . that was it! It was the superbly innovative writing that prompted my erstwhile euphoria. Thank God for that I thought; I'm not completely at fault. There was also the problem with the electricity . . . Of course. Anyone accomplishing anything remotely near the quality of those six pages, with the clever and intricate plot scenario, would have good reason to sink a pint or two. I reached over to my jacket pocket to find the papers; to read through it again; that would prove exactly how justified I was in having indulged in a mild celebration.

No matter how many times I checked the pockets it still wasn't there. I undid the black plastic bag where I'd placed my vomit covered jeans and searched through the pockets. No . . . still nothing. Oh Christ, this is unbelievable, I thought. Another frantic look around the room only confirmed my worst fears. I'd left it in the pub!

'Well at least I know where it is' I said to myself. 'It's not exactly lost. That delightful young barmaid will have picked it up and put it in a safe place for me.' It was now nine thirty. In another hour the pub would be opening, I'd just saunter in, and she would smile that broad electrifying smile of hers and say, 'Oh I think this must be yours,' and hand it to me without me even having to say anything. Thank God for that!

I'd been sitting on the bed day dreaming now for the past ten minutes about my mislaid manuscript and the barmaid . . . well . . . mainly the barmaid to be truthful. I was contemplating the enormous challenges that struggling writers have to overcome, when a loud bang, bang, bang, on my door caused me to jump out of my skin.

I got up off the bed slowly, walked over and opened it. There facing me like some terrifying apparition was the man who'd been following me.

"Jesus . . . Jesus Christ," I said instinctively. "What do you want?"

"Sorry to disturb you," he said, "my name is Vince; Vincent Stubbs. We're neighbours so to speak. I thought I'd introduce myself, and at the same time I promised

Mrs Hoskins that I'd give you a knock. She's a bit worried as you didn't show for dinner last night, or at breakfast this morning."

I was completely frozen to the spot. My heart was racing; I was soaked in perspiration. My mouth was so dry, I could hardly speak. My headache returned instantly. I wished to God this was just a terrible dream I was having, but knew it wasn't.

"What do you mean 'neighbours?'" I asked hearing my voice quivering.

"I've rented the room next door, that's all I meant."

"Why?" I asked. "Why have you rented the room? What is it you want?"

Mr Vincent Stubbs ignored these questions: "Alright, well I won't keep you; I'll let Mrs Hoskins know you're fine on my way out. Perhaps . . . we can have a little chat together sometime . . . this evening even . . . if that's okay with you. I feel sure we'll find a lot to talk about." He then turned and slowly descended the stairs leaving me transfixed by the doorway watching him.

I was now visibly shaking. No one could now suggest that this was some figment of my imagination. I retreated back into the room and locked the door. I was going over in my mind what he'd just said, and the menacing way he'd said: *'I feel sure we'll find a lot to talk about'*.

What was this all about? Something had to be done. . . Urgently. I thought again about what Julia had said, about going to the police. I ran through it in my mind: So okay; I go to the police station and explain the whole thing. This man . . . yes I know his name now. This man Vincent Stubbs has been following me for the past five days. Now he's rented the room next to me and wants us to have a chat. Hmm . . . sounds completely ludicrous. They're hardly going to send out some specially trained snatch squad to come out and pick him up are they? Chances are they'll think I need some psychiatric help. They're bound to say that this should be seen as a friendly gesture . . . a neighbourly thing to do. No, no, I can't do that; it would make me sound paranoid. Apart from that: just supposing the police did come round here and question him. That would make things worse. Mrs Hoskins would think I was some sort of trouble maker, or more likely, would assume that I'd finally gone mad. She obviously thinks there's something strange about me anyway. Particularly after having dragged her out yesterday in the pouring rain to show her the man that was following me; the man that *wasn't* actually there! No, one thing is certain; I can't go to the police.

After reasoning my way through this I was mildly relieved that under the circumstances I was still able to make logical and rational decisions. Well . . . as far as calling the police was concerned. This though, was only *one* line of thought. It didn't solve the conundrum. Perhaps there was an innocent explanation after all. It could be that he's just lonely. Mrs Hoskins did say he was a very nice man who'd lost his wife. Yes, of course that could easily be it. The poor chap's just grieving and desperately needs somebody to talk to. I remembered how difficult it was when Julia and I broke up. We'd only been together six months, but that awful feeling of loss . . . yes it can be very difficult. It doesn't explain why he'd been following me though. Unless he thought he knew me, or maybe . . . maybe he thought I was somebody else. And so my unsatisfactory ruminations continued.

I was in for yet another shock. My optimistic assumption that the barmaid in the Crown and Anchor would smile affectionately and produce my manuscript was misguided. She hadn't seen it and didn't have a clue what I was talking about. Despite my anguished and insistent protestations; that it *must* be in there somewhere. Although the cleaners had long since left, I carried out a desperate search under all the tables and chairs, refusing to believe that it wasn't there. Finally I announced bitterly that somebody must have sto en it and left.

This was all Jack's fault I concluded standing outside the pub. Had he not fused the lights, I wouldn't have needed to go to the pub in the first place. There must be some conspiracy going on. Yes, that's what it is; everyone around me was conspiring against me. What had I done to *them?* I'd made enough sacrifices; all I wanted to do now was to be left in peace to write my book: but *they* wouldn't let me. 'Bastards', I muttered, walking off in the direction of the town centre.

With no particular plan in mind, I carried on walking. The sun was shining; the sky a dense blue with not a cloud to be seen. The wind had abated and in every respect it was just like a spring day. On the verge of despair; I was thinking about phoning Julia. She would offer some comforting words to ease my suffering. There were though a number of problems with this idea: the first and foremost objection to this; would be that she would interpret this as a sign of weakness. She would sense that I was having recriminations about my writing aspirations; that I'd made the wrong decision, and was trying to make amends. The second, almost equally important, it would necessitate another visit to 'The Copper Kettle'. Thirdly, she might have already agreed to meet somebody for lunch, and in my fragile state of mind, I'd have to handle the rejection.

I walked on for a further five hundred yards and decided the most sensible thing to do would be to go straight back to my typewriter and try and re-construct the lost pages. The longer I left it; the more difficult it would become. Yes, I mustn't be defeated; it's only a minor set back after all: I muttered trying to convince myself.

Passing the pub on the way back, I started feeling queasy and slightly faint. At first I thought that this was caused by the smell of stale beer, and home cooked food wafting out of the doorway. It then dawned on me that I'd eaten nothing since my meagre breakfast yesterday morning. I must have lost three stone since then. I stopped dead in my tracks for a few moments contemplating a further visit to the pub. I was starving hungry and seriously dehydrated. Why not go in there and have a pint and a plate of hot savoury home cooked something or other? It wasn't a difficult decision to make: a few moments later I was sitting at the same table with a dark golden coloured pint in front of me and a plate of shepherd's pie on its way.

To pass the time I picked up a newspaper that someone had left on the chair next to me. Thumbing through it I stopped at the 'books' section. I was drawn to the adverts from the major book sellers promoting 'Celebrity Memoirs'. The affect of this prompted an instantaneous regression in my mood. Multi-million pound sales of books entitled 'My Life', My Story, etc, books 'written' by nineteen year olds that in truth have experienced nothing, and couldn't string a single sentence together to save their lives. 'Bastards', I said to myself: how can agents dare call themselves 'literary agents' when they contaminate themselves with this. What's 'literary' about this load of garbage! Let's face it they're all philistines: money, money, money . . . that's what it's all about. Well, I said to myself, as the hot steaming shepherd's pie was thumped down on the table: let's hope that one of them is able to recognise pure literary genius when 'One murder too many' by Tom Dunford is slapped on their desks!

Having devoured the shepherd's pie and another pint, I was overcome with tiredness. My eyelids were drooping; the chair was soft and comfortable; I could have easily just sat there and nodded off. The warm congenial atmosphere of the saloon bar was in stark contrast to my cold dingy room. I knew though, that the sooner I got back to my typewriter and re-captured the lost words, the better I'd feel.

Gazing around me outside the pub, I was troubled with feelings of foreboding at the thought of going back to my room. What had hitherto been a peaceful, albeit austere environment had changed. The prospect of 'Vince' whoever he was, being now so close to me was disturbing. Why was everything becoming so bloody difficult?

After three hours I'd typed out as much as I could remember of the first draft and read through it several times. Okay, it wasn't exactly word for word the same, but it looked reasonably good. I now had to make up lost ground; I'd not produced anything in the last twenty fours hours which was lamentable. In another two hours dinner would be served. Oh Christ, I thought . . . dinner . . . Vince . . . he's likely to be there . . . he's a 'half boarder', that's what she'd said . . . Oh bloody hell; this wretched person . . . this weird sinister character is going to be sitting there in the bloody dining room. I lighted a cigarette and sat on the edge of the bed; again trying to make some sense of it. Torturing myself; I recounted what had been happening from the first day I became aware of being followed. However hard I tried to explain and justify 'Vince's' behaviour, my attempts at self deception offered little amelioration. For the past few hours I'd been absorbed with recapturing my lost work. Now with just over an hour to go before dinner; I was beginning to panic. I felt trapped, isolated and vulnerable: the two top attic rooms were close together. I couldn't go in or out without passing Vince's room. Oh well . . . Perhaps after a friendly chat, all will become clear. He probably is just lonely and has a problem making friends. He certainly didn't look like a madman; he was well dressed . . . and . . . and why on earth would he be interested in me? No; what a fool I am; I've blown this whole thing up out of proportion, ha-ha, that's it of course.

I paced around the room for another ten minutes, feeling relieved that things weren't as bad as they seemed. The book; *this* book was going to be a winner; an overnight success. It had all the right ingredients; I wasn't a fool, I knew what I was doing. The publishers would be crying out for a sequel; all I'd have to do would be to name the price. I'd look back in a few years time and laugh at all of this. Teething problems, that's what they were . . . little obstacles that many writers have had to face.

At five to seven I wandered down to the dining room. All the usual faces were firmly positioned at their tables. Benson gave me a friendly nod and held a thumb up whilst grinning inanely. I returned the thumbs up sign which at least obviated the requirement to speak, and walked over to my table. I immediately registered that there was no sign of 'Vince'.

The meal being served tonight was spaghetti bolognaise; not one of Mrs Hoskins' better dishes. The pasta was always overcooked, soggy and floating in water. The sauce was anaemic, virtually tasteless. The point was, that having missed the last two meals; I had to put in an appearance to prevent her delving too deeply into what I was up to; failing to turn up for three meals would invariably result in a well meaning but nonetheless monotonous lecture, about young people nowadays, the importance of looking after yourself and so on. Oh Christ; anything to avoid this!

I pulled the newspaper that I'd picked up in the pub from my pocket and unfolded it. As I held it out in front of me I glimpsed Vince walking across the dining room. He looked around at the other residents and then focused in on me. Our eyes met, but I quickly looked straight down into my newspaper again. I was aware from the corner of my eye that he'd had stopped near my table momentarily, presumably hoping for some verbal acknowledgement. When I sensed that he'd moved to a table directly out of my line of vision, I folded the paper again and propped it up on the table. I placed my elbows on the table and both hands against my temples as if to create blinkers, and started reading . . . well, pretending to read. I wasn't quite sure where he was sitting, but I knew I must avoid any further possible eye to eye contact with him.

"Are you alright dear now?" Mrs Hoskins enquired as she placed a portion of her gastronomic delicacy and some apple pie and custard in front of me, "only Mr Benson said you weren't feeling too good last night."

"Yes, I'm fine Mrs Hoskins thank you."

"Well, you must eat regularly; I know what you young people are like. You're always so busy you forget to eat and then you wonder why you start getting ill."

"No really I'm fine, it was just a tummy upset."
Benson looked over towards me and winked. He of course knew better.

I didn't waste any time. The spaghetti was only lukewarm. Within five minutes I'd swallowed the lot. I then scooped up the apple pie and custard with accomplished dexterity and immediately got up from the table. I wanted to get back up to my room and avoid any mid stairs encounters with Vince, or anyone else for that matter.

Four minutes later I was safely back in my room sitting in front of the typewriter blowing smoke rings up against the window. Apart from slight indigestion from bolting the food so rapidly, I was feeling much better. Vince wasn't going to worry me; the writing was going to take precedence; now I would make up for lost time and start chapter twelve. I'd been typing away for about an hour when a bang, bang, bang on the door made me jump out of my skin. I got up and opened it. There standing outside was Vincent Stubbs.

"I'd like you and me to have a little chat," he said without smiling.

"A little chat . . . about what?"

"I've got some pictures . . . some photographs, I think you might be interested in seeing."

"What photographs? What do you mean?"

"Well, I can hardly show them to you standing here on the landing can I? I thought we might have a little drink together at the same," he said, pulling a half bottle of scotch out of his coat pocket and holding in front of me.

I felt an icy chill go through me. I was terrified. My worst fears had materialised. This didn't sound friendly. The intimidating and menacing way this man spoke to me was indicative of something worse to come. What would happen should I refuse? Was this even an option? Overcome with fear and panic I tried, "I'm sorry," I said, without being able to think clearly. "I'm very busy this evening, another time I . . ."

Before I could complete the sentence, he'd pushed past me and was in my room. "Got a couple of glasses have you?" he asked.

Realizing that I had little choice I produced two half pint pewter tankards which Mrs Hoskins had left as ornaments on the mantelpiece, and held them up towards him.

"Well aren't you going to close the door?" he said, "It's cold enough in here anyway, without the bloody door being open."

I walked over to the door wondering if I should just run down the stairs and out into the street whilst I had the chance. No this would be a ridiculously spineless move, I thought, and closed the door.

"Aren't you going to invite me to sit down?"

"Yes of course," I said, trying to steady my voice.

"These are clean I take it," he said, lifting up one of the tankards.

"Yes . . . yes they are. I don't have many visitors but when . . ."

"Don't worry," he interrupted, "we're all going to die of something soon anyway, and a bit it of dust, a few dead flies hardly matter. Mrs Hoskins tells me you're a writer," he said, whilst emptying half the bottle carefully between the two tankards.

"Yes, that's right."

"Been a writer long have you?"

"No, only for a few months. I'm trying to write a best seller; a murder mystery, you know that sort of thing."

"Make any money at it, do you?"

"Well, I've had a few things published: articles, short stories, nothing very praise worthy, but I think now I'm on the right track," I said, hoping that this open friendly reply would ease the situation a bit.

Ignoring this feeble attempt at dissimulation, he then opened the large brown envelope he'd been holding and took out some photographs.

"Ah yes, Mrs Hoskins told me that you're a photographer," I said, still trying desperately to instigate a normal conversation.

"Take a look at this," he said, handing me a large coloured photo of an expensive looking country house.

"Gosh, yes, that's a nice photograph. There's no doubt you've had plenty of practice with a camera."

"Right now take a look at this," he continued, handing me a photograph of an attractive looking woman in the garden of the same house.

"Oh yes, she's an attractive looking woman. Is she . . . Oh I'm really sorry, I meant was this your wife? Mrs Hoskins did tell me that sadly you lost your wife a few years ago; and the little girl sitting next to her . . . is that . . . is that your daughter?"

Stubbs made no reply. He stared menacingly at me for a full five seconds. He lifted his tankard of scotch and pointed it at me.

"Have a drink," he said. "You're going to need it before I show you the rest."

I lifted my tankard finding it difficult to stop my hand from trembling and took a sip of gritty tasting whisky.

"Cheers," I said, pitifully aware of my breaking voice, frantically trying to anticipate what was to follow.

He downed the contents of his tankard and refilled both his and mine with the remaining half bottle. He then picked up the brown envelope and withdrew some more photos.

"Right, now have at look at this one," he said, thrusting a further photo in front of me.

The picture showed the charred remains of a burned out house.

"Good God," I said, the second I focused on it. "Is this the same property? This wasn't your house by any chance, was it?"

He didn't reply. He stared at me for another extremely uncomfortable five seconds and handed me another photo. This one was even more bizarre and spine chilling. A picture of a headstone. On it was inscribed:

17th March 1930----------Passed away 3rd June 1975
In loving memory of Claire Anne Stubbs. Wife of
Vincent and mother of Janice.

I was finding it difficult to contain my fear. Dreading to think what all this could be leading to; and what the hell was going to come next.

"Oh I am really sorry," I said, "That's obviously your wife's memorial stone. How did she die?"

He ignored this question. He took the photo back and handed me another. This one was of the little girl. Her face, arms and legs horribly disfigured. I felt sickened just looking at it.

"God, that's truly awful. What happened to her?"

"She got badly burned in the fire. My wife died in the fire trying to save her. She's still alive, but as you can see the skin on her face just melted like plastic."

"Oh God this is terrible, I really am terribly sorry; you've suffered a terrible misfortune. When did all this happen?"

"Five years ago in 1975 . . . but wait . . . I've got one more thing to show you."

He reached into the envelope and took out a letter: carefully unfolded it and handed it to me. "Read this," he said.

The letter was from The Commercial Protection Insurance Company. It was worded as follows:

"Dear Mr Stubbs,
We have re-examined the facts relating to your claim in respect of fire and contents insurance covered by this policy, and regret to inform you that we stand by our original decision in that an untruthful declaration contained in your initial proposal renders this policy void."

The letter was signed by Tom Dunford. Claims Manager.

Chapter 3

I stared at the letter in disbelief. Yes, it was definitely my signature; but I had no recollection of writing it, or for that matter anything to do with the case. I read through it again shaking my head as if I couldn't understand such gross injustice.

"Yes, this is obviously my signature, but I really can't remember this particular case, or why this decision was made."

He fixed an icy penetrating stare on me. A vein above his right eye appeared to enlarge and was visibly throbbing. As his face reddened with suppressed anger, another vein above his left eye accompanied it.

"The decision was made my friend, because I signed a declaration when the insurance was taken out, saying that I hadn't made any claims within the last five years. I genuinely thought that a claim I had made for a broken toilet cistern was *over* five years ago. It turned out that it was exactly four years, eleven months and twenty six days from the date I signed this declaration. This was the excuse you used for not paying out on the policy."

"If that was so," I said, slowly getting up from the chair, "Then although it might seem terribly unjust: the company would have been within its rights in refusing to pay out."

He sprung off his chair in a fit of rage and grabbed me by the lapels of my jacket forcing me up against the wall. Although he was probably twenty years older than me; he was at least a head taller and powerfully built. I didn't just *feel* inadequate: I knew I was; and certainly no match for the terrifying onslaught that was about to be unleashed.

"Quite within its rights eh? What did you say, you fucking little shit? Quite within its rights was it? Well let me tell you something," he said, shaking me, and banging the back of my head repeatedly against the wall. "It's going to be quite within *my* fucking rights to tear your fucking head off."

He released me with a violent push forcing me to almost lose my balance and stagger back against the wall. He then sat down again; his face contorting into a strange grimace as he put his hands over his face and started crying uncontrollably. I stood where I was, completely petrified with shock and disbelief.

After what seemed an eternity of him sobbing and wailing in the chair; I tried to creep past him to the door to escape; he jumped up and ordered me to sit down.

"Look, I'm sorry. I really am so sorry . . . I"

"Shut up," he shouted. "You've ruined my life. Do you think it wasn't bad enough losing my wife in the fire, and having my precious little daughter scarred for life? Do you think that wasn't fucking bad enough . . . without you making it worse? I'd put every penny I ever earned into that house; every penny. It was worth nearly half a million. On top of that I lost my studio, my business, everything. I was a very successful photographer; I lost my cameras and all my equipment. One day I had everything: then suddenly everything was taken away from me."

"What caused the fire?" I asked, hoping this question would not promote a further violent tirade.

"No one ever found out, they thought it might have been due to an electrical fault; but the cause was never discovered. At first the fire investigators thought that it might have been an arson attempt. There were three cans of petrol in the barn that was attached to the house; petrol that I used for our lawn mowers. Of course you were delighted at this . . . thought you were off the hook . . . a way out for you not to pay up. This theory couldn't be substantiated; there was no other evidence, and obviously no motive. Why would I want to burn my own fucking house down? The whole thing was quite ridiculous . . . grasping at straws . . . any reason not to pay out. When this failed, you went through the small print; checked the claims history . . . and found what you were looking for."

I gazed at him for a few seconds, frantically trying to think of another question to keep him talking; hoping that the more he got off his chest the calmer he might become.

"It really is a terrible story," I said. "I just don't know what to say. All I can tell you is that all insurance companies work in much the same way. It's nothing personal. Some fires are obviously started deliberately. The insurance companies have to exclude this possibility before paying out on a policy. There are also quite a high percentage of people who lie about their previous claims history knowing that if they told the truth they either wouldn't get cover: or if they did, that the premiums would be much higher."

Not being adept in the art of tact and diplomacy, my comment incited him into another fit of rage. He stared at me for a few seconds; his face an unhealthy crimson colour with the veins in his forehead swelling and pulsating dramatically. He leapt up from the chair and sprung on me like a panther on its prey. I tried to get up and run to the door again but wasn't quick enough. He grabbed me by the hair and the lapels of my jacket and pulled me out of the chair, lifted me up and swung me around forcing me up against the wall. I was terrified, I couldn't get my breath. I screwed my eyes shut; too frightened to look into the angry face of my attacker; praying that whatever was going to happen to me now would be over quickly.

"Some of them lie do they?" He said, contorting his face into an ugly grimace as he released the words. "Some of them lie, that's what you just said wasn't it? You fucking loathsome piece of shit." He slapped me across the face twice with the back of his hand and shook me: still holding me by the lapels of my jacket. "Well I didn't fucking lie . . . right?" I then felt an excruciating pain as I was kneed in the groin: causing me to double over and writhe on the floor in agony with my hands between my legs. "Well," he said placing a foot on my head, "you should have been more careful to find out who some of these people are that you refer to as liars. Some of them may not be liars at all. Some of them are decent honest people that can't remember exact fucking dates . . . and you . . . you little shit . . . choose to completely fuck their lives up. Don't worry, I'm not going to kill you this evening; this is just what you might call an introduction into what pain and suffering is all about. Or to put it more succinctly . . . the pain and suffering that you've caused. "Do you understand?" he shouted. "Do you fucking understand?"

"Yes, yes," I groaned.

"Don't misunderstand me," he continued. "The physical pain you felt then is temporary. In an hour or so it'll pass. The pain you experience in losing a loved one doesn't pass . . . it goes on. This is the sort of pain I want you to experience you fucking little shit. No, don't worry; I'm not going to kill you . . . that would be too easy. I'm not letting you get off that easily. I'm going to wait. I've waited five years; and I'll wait a little bit longer. The only way you'll ever understand what I'm talking about is when you lose somebody *you* love."

I was now sitting up on the floor whimpering and rocking with pain with him standing over me.

"What is it you want?" I said. "I've told you, I'm sorry; I really don't know what else to say. If I could make it up to you in some way . . . believe me . . . I would."

"Get up, and sit there," he demanded, pointing to the chair he had just dragged me from. "Come on . . . fucking get up."

I found it almost too painful to move. Very slowly I got up from the floor and taking small half steps fell into the chair.

He moved his chair directly opposite and sat down facing me.

"As I was saying the only way you're going to understand how I feel is when *you* lose the person closest to you."

"I understood what you were saying."

"Good." He said. "I thought you were going to get married a while ago . . . you disappointed me."

"Christ, how did you know that? What do you mean, I disappointed you?"

"Think about it. Think about what I just said."

"Look, the fact that your house was destroyed, the death of your wife and the injury's your daughter suffered . . . is tragic beyond doubt: I do understand . . . really I do, but surely you can't blame me for that."

"Of course I don't," he confirmed. "The point is that had you not behaved like a pernickety little shitbag; I would have at least received the insurance money. This wouldn't have compensated in any way for the loss of my wife, or the dreadful injury's my daughter sustained, but it would have helped me to cope; to start trying to rebuild my life. I needn't have lost everything. I ended up on the street without a pot to piss in. I couldn't even look after my daughter; I was completely destitute. This; all of this, is quite definitely your fault. Do you not agree?"

Whether I agreed or not, was irrelevant. I knew now exactly the sort of reaction any argument to the contrary would provoke. I was beginning to accept that he had a point. In all the years I'd worked for the insurance company, I'd never actually thought about real people; real lives, the physical and emotional distress that my decisions might cause. Technically of course I was probably right. But morally: . . . the more I thought about it, the harder it became to justify my actions. How on earth could it be 'fair' that for what was an innocent mistake . . . miscalculating a few days over a five year period, a man should lose everything?

"I have to agree with you," I said. "To be honest, I've never thought about what happens outside the walls of the insurance office. There isn't even a grey area when one considers the facts of this case as you have explained them. It's hardly likely that anyone in your position would have had any reason not to disclose the truth. I really am sorry. The whole claim should have been dealt with more sympathetically; the company should have paid out on the claim, even if they reduced the payout by a small percentage in view of the error."

"I wonder how many other people's lives you've fucked up," he said.

I didn't want to think about this. I'd been indoctrinated by my peers at an early age. Conditioned to believe that most claimants are low life scum; most of them examples of 'the something for nothing' leech ethos that preys upon society. According to my departmental manager, more than half the claims coming in were 'fabricated'. 'We are living in a greedy compensation culture', he told me, 'where every claim, if not directly fraudulent; will never be *exactly* as stated'. It would be my job eventually, to go through each case that exceeded a certain amount of money, and dissect it, and everything about it, with the finest of toothcombs. Find the flaw; find the obvious lie, some minor discrepancy in the application . . . anything that would negate the claim. The more I thought about this, the more I sympathized with him.

"Where is your daughter now?" I asked apprehensively; terrified that he would fly into yet another uncontrollable rage.

Taking another slurp of the fly contaminated whisky, he slowly placed the tankard on the floor and stared at me; his eyes darkened with hatred.

"She's with my sister. Without my sister I would have topped myself. She's been an angel. After the fire, I stayed with her. Janice was in hospital for nearly six months having skin grafts and plastic surgery. I couldn't have worked even if I could have found a job. The doctors said I was suffering from post traumatic stress disorder; I was heavily sedated and was wandering around like a fucking zombie. I used to visit her in hospital and after each operation, I just used to walk along the beach here crying my eyes out. When Janice came out I couldn't stand to look at her: her beautiful little face was destroyed. It seemed to me that despite the good intentions of the doctors and hospital staff, that they were making her worse. In the end I got a job as a press photographer for a newspaper in California. I borrowed some money from my sister, and somehow managed to get a visa and went over there. They were very good to me after I explained what had happened. They even gave me some money to buy a camera and some equipment. I enjoyed working for them, they were decent people. For a while I managed to keep it together, sending money back to my sister, and naively imagining that at some point Janice would be well enough to come over and join me; but this really was a ridiculous dream. After three years the newspaper folded. I managed to survive with the help of some contacts I'd made, doing wedding photos, portraits, that sort of thing; but I wasn't earning enough to keep body and soul together. In the end I had what is euphemistically called a nervous breakdown. I spent a couple of months in a psychiatric hospital, and then came back here. I decided that all the time I'd been in denial. The only way through it, was for me to find and confront the fucking little piece of shit that caused all this unnecessary suffering. There is only one thing I want now and that's retribution. It's the only way I'll ever find any peace."

I felt a chill of fear. A fear I never imagined possible. The most bizarre thoughts were racing through my mind. This man was seriously unhinged. For a few moments whilst he was talking I imagined that he was just unwinding . . . getting things off his chest. I could now see this was not the case. He was seriously deranged and dangerous.

"What form of retribution? You're no doubt asking yourself. Well this is a very good question that I've been asking myself for the past five years. The first thing I wanted to do was to find you, and talk to you face to face. To see what sort of a little scumbag you actually were. You're not exactly as I'd pictured you . . . if anything you're even more pathetic. I wasn't sure if I'd be compelled to kill you on our first meeting. I was hoping I'd be able to find some inner strength and restrain myself. I would be failing my duty if I simply killed you; that wouldn't provide the satisfaction I'm looking for. I need you to share my suffering; the suffering you have caused. The only way this can be achieved is for you to lose the person you love.

"But I have no one. My parents split up when I was a teenager and I haven't kept in contact with either of them. I don't have any brothers or sisters; I'm completely on my own."

"Yes that might be true at the moment," he said, "but what about Julia?"

"Christ, what do you mean 'Julia'? How did you know about her?"

"Don't underestimate me you little shit. I know all I need to know."

"Julia and I split up four months ago: She and I aren't together anymore."

"No, you may not be at the moment, but that's something I intend to keep an eye on. When I saw the pair of you the other day, you didn't exactly behave like strangers."

"Christ, I think you need help," I said without thinking. "I can cope with you threatening my life, but . . . Julia . . . she's had nothing to do with this. This is . . ."

"I think you're now beginning to understand aren't you?"

"Has it not crossed your mind that I might go to the police?"

"It's crossed my mind of course. But what do you suppose the police are going to do? All that I can see is that I've rented a room next door to you, and you and I have just had a little neighbourly chat together. I think it might be nice instead if we deal with this in a friendly manner. Perhaps you ought to introduce me to Julia. We've not actually spoken to each other yet. Why don't I suggest the three of us have lunch in 'The Copper Kettle', I know that's a favourite of hers."

"Look," I said trying desperately to steer him away from Julia: "going back to what you were saying . . . you know . . . the injustice . . . the way you were treated by the insurance company and . . ."

"Not the insurance company. By you . . . you fucking little creep."

"Okay, okay, I'm sorry, I've already admitted that it was wrong haven't I? The point is I'd like to make it up to you if I possibly can."

"What do you mean, 'make it up to me' I'm not a shirt lifter, if that's what you're thinking you fucking little wretch."

"Oh for Christ's sake. What I was going to say is that I'm writing a book: I think it could be successful. I've sent off the first three chapters and a synopsis to my agents, and they seem to think it could stand a pretty good chance of being published. I don't know how much you know about the book trade, but this is what every writer dreams about. It's possible . . . just possible that it could be a best seller. If it is, I could be paid a considerable advance; not just for this one, but for sequels as well. Well what I'm trying to say is that you can have the money . . . all of it. I mean it. I honestly feel dreadful thinking about what's happened to you, and I agree it was my fault . . . the claim . . . the money should have been paid out to you. I agree entirely. At least this would give me a chance to make good some of the damage I've caused you. I know it might only be a token, but it could be enough to get you on your feet again."

"Hmm, you think this is going to get you off the hook do you?"

"It's not like that at all; I know you're upset; I'm sure I'd feel exactly the same. I genuinely want to do something to help. You've experienced a great injustice, and I do feel responsible. I don't have any money right now that I could give you, but this is something I'd like to do."

"It's fascinating watching you squirm, you little shit. I like the idea though. How long do you think it will take you to complete it?"

"Well, it's hard to say exactly . . .I've got about another six chapters to write; so far its taking about a week for each one, so something like another six weeks or so should see the first draft completed. I'd expect to spend another couple of weeks on it, tidying up loose ends, making corrections, that sort of thing, so probably about two months."

"And how much are we talking about? How much do you expect to get for it?"

"Well that really is impossible to know. It may be that it comes to nothing after all. I'm quite prepared for that, although I don't think that's going to be the case. I have just got to put that side of it completely out of my mind and write as well as I can."

"Right, so what you're offering me is just sophistry; some nebulous dream of yours in the hope that I'd be stupid enough to swallow it. What do you propose to do if the book isn't published? Do you think I'm going to sit around patiently waiting while you write another one?" Stubbs paused, obviously considering something. "I think though, I will be fairer with you, than you have been with me. I'll give you the two months you say you need, and let's hope for your sake the book is a success. If it's not, don't expect me to make allowances for you. You're going to be given one chance, and only one chance: so in effect you'll be writing to save your life; yes ha-ha, I like that."

"Well, I'll do the best I can," I said; overwhelmed with relief that at least some form of accommodation had finally been reached with this madman.

"There will be a few restrictions and proviso's on this little arrangement," he continued. "Firstly: you are to stay exactly where you are . . . in this room . . . in this house. I'll continue to occupy the room next door. I intend to keep an eye on you. I want weekly progress reports until the book is finished. I want to see all the correspondence you send out and receive: and don't misunderstand me, two months, means two months; not a day longer. Is that quite clear?"

"Yes, yes of course," I said, grateful that however nefarious and bizarre these instructions were, at least he seemed content for the moment.

"Right, I think that just about concludes our little discussion for this evening. For the moment you've got a reprieve. If you attempt to talk to anyone, and you know what I mean by that, or try and fuck with me in any way, I'll find you. Make no mistake, I'll fucking kill you and her as well. Is that absolutely clear?" He said, poking a finger in my face.

"Don't worry, I understand."

He turned around, walked slowly towards the door, paused for a few moments; fixed a long penetrating stare on me, and left. I sat where I was trembling like a leaf; I listened and heard the key enter the door to the room next to him, the door open and then click shut. I felt trapped like a frightened animal. I got up slowly and tiptoed over to my door and very carefully drew the bolt across. Pressing my ear to the door, I tried to hear whether he was moving around.

Traumatized and still trembling, I crept back and sat down again, picked up my tankard of whisky which I'd hardly touched and drank a large mouthful. I spluttered and coughed as the whisky burned the back of my throat. I desperately wanted to run, to escape; but where? The police . . . I must *now* go to the police. Not only was my life in danger; this raving madman had set his sights on Julia as well. What was happening to me? This was a terrifying nightmare. What if the police didn't believe me? There were no witnesses, no evidence, and no proof. They would surely question him if any allegations were made, and he'd deny it. Not only that: he would then unleash a manic tirade of violence against me, and probably kill me, or even worse, maim me for life. No, I couldn't go to the police. But hang on . . . what about the attack . . . he had after all physically attacked me; surely that would mean they'd *have* to do something. But no, they wouldn't: what proof was there? There were no marks on me, no cuts, and no bruises. I did now have balls the size of coconuts, but wasn't particularly keen on exposing them as evidence. Why should they believe me? I thought of running . . . (no, perhaps more like waddling, in my present condition) out of the house and going round to Julia's flat; but then realized this would be completely pointless: he'd been watching Julia; no doubt he knew where she lived; he would probably then turn up in the middle of the night and kill both of us. 'Just sit tight and think about it', I kept telling myself. At the moment, he's unlikely to do anything, provided I stick to the plan. Two months . . .

he's not going to do anything for two months, I said to myself. If I can somehow continue to write, finish the book, that'll keep him on a reasonably stable path. I mustn't think beyond that. Hopefully the book will sell, I'll give him the money, and that'll be it.

It was nearly midnight; my ordeal had gone on for almost three hours. I was putting off a much needed trip across the hallway to the bathroom, for fear of bumping into him. The excruciating pain from my testicles had travelled up to my stomach. Eventually I opened my door as quietly as I could and tiptoed across the freezing passage to the bathroom. The relief of getting back safely to my room was immeasurable. I thought about getting undressed but felt too vulnerable. What if he should burst into the room in the middle of the night? The pain in my groin was definitely getting worse. At three o'clock I got undressed and tried to get a few hours sleep. At five o'clock I had given up hope. In another two hours the loose pane of glass would be rattling in the window, and it would be approaching breakfast time. Oh God . . . the dining room . . . I thought . . . Stubbs: Oh bloody hell, I must find a way of dealing with this, I told myself. If this goes on much longer it'll be me that ends up in a psychiatric hospital.

A few moments later I had a sudden flash of inspiration. Why not incorporate him into my next book! The whole story could be an exact description of what I was going through. This would have real impact . . . it must! After all it would be written with first hand experience. I sat up and thought about it . . . yes this would be an excellent plot for a novel, and then a cold shiver went through me as I thought about how it might end.

With much trepidation I took some mincing steps down to the dining room, deciding that I must try to conceal the fear that now penetrated every fibre of my being. As I approached my table Mrs Hoskins rushed over to me and announced that 'a gentleman' had been waiting in the visitors lounge to see me. I thanked her and poked my head around the door and spotted Clive, an old friend sitting there reading a newspaper.

"Clive," I shouted, "what brings you here?"

"Hello mate, how are things? I was going to walk up to your room but Mrs Hoskins said you'd be down any minute now, so I thought I'd save my legs. Doesn't that finish you off, that climb up and down all the time?"

"No, you've got to be fit to live here," I said, my grey pallor and bloodshot eyes not exactly supporting the intended inference.

"The reason I popped by is that it's Rachel's birthday today; we're going to go out for a few drinks and a curry, and wondered if you'd like to join us? We were just saying we haven't seen you for a while: well not since you and Julia split up . . . oh how is she by the way? Do you still keep in touch?"

"Yes I'd love to: Julia? Yes she's fine; we do bump into each other occasionally but that's as far as it goes."

"Pity, we used to get on so well together . . . the four of us."

"Yes, I know, but these things happen."

"Do you think you two will ever get back together?"

"Who knows? At the moment I'm determined to continue with my book. I've got a deadline now to finish it."

"How come, has somebody made you an offer you can't refuse?"

"You might say that."

"Oh well, you can tell us all about this evening, we'll see you in the pub over the road about eight if that's okay. I must rush; I should have been at work ten minutes ago."

"Okay," I said, hoping that the pain in my groin would ease as the day went on, "see you this evening."

I managed to avoid any direct eye contact with Stubbs as I walked through the dining room to my table. He was concentrating on a newspaper spread over the table in front of him. I deliberately sat with my back to him, took out a cigarette and poured myself a cup of weak tea. From where I was sitting I could just make out the reflection of him in the glass doors of the welsh dresser in front of me.

"Did you see the young gentleman?" Mrs Hoskins enquired, as she placed two slices of pale looking toast in front of me.

I immediately noticed Stubbs look up from the paper and glare at me. Who was the young gentleman Mrs Hoskins was referring to? Was this 'young gentleman' from the police? Were these the thoughts going through his mind? Is this why he looked up so quickly? I asked myself. My heart was racing, palms sweating. Is this innocent visit going to precipitate this madman bursting into my room and kneeing me in the groin again? The very thought of it made my eyes water.

"Yes I did thanks Mrs Hoskins. It was an old pal of mine; we're going out tonight to celebrate his girlfriends birthday," I replied in a voice loud enough for everyone to hear in the hope that this might just allay Stubbs's suspicions.

I finished my breakfast as quickly as I could; checked the reflection to make sure that Stubbs was not just about to leave; got up and crept back to my room locking the door behind me. Although the room wasn't warm, the sweat was pouring off me; my hands were shaking causing me to miss keys as I typed. The constant pounding of my heart made me wonder if I was about to have a heart attack. I stopped for a moment and wrung my hands together trying to squeeze away the nervous tension that they contained. Eventually I regained some composure; the words were beginning to flow once more. I'd worked out that I needed to write at least a thousand words a day for the next six weeks. If I produced anything less than this, then I could be in trouble. I consoled myself by declaring that if I could manage to write under such oppressive circumstances, then I must definitely have a talent for it. Once this book was finished, and hopefully published, I'd have Stubbs off my back, and would have really established myself as a writer. The rest of it would be easy, I could then write at a more leisurely pace without these constant threats and intimidation.

As the day wore on tiredness got the better of me. By lunchtime I'd produced four pages, which by my estimation must have been just over a thousand words. I read and re-read what was sitting in front of me. The more I read it, the more amateurish it sounded. 'Ch hell,

I mumbled to myself; 'how the devil is anyone expected to write under these conditions?' A further half an hour passed in which I was finding it difficult to focus. The words I did manage to read didn't seem to make any sense. Perhaps some fresh air might help, I thought . . . a short walk . . .go out and find something to eat . . .a sandwich and some strong coffee . . .that might help.

After five whole minutes with my ear pressed against the door, I convinced myself that Stubbs wasn't about to come flying out of his room, and that it was safe to leave. The grey soulless sky and a sharp wind cutting into me as I walked into the street was a stark reminder that a cruel cold winter was on its way. The sandwich bar I occasionally frequented was at least three hundred yards up the road, but now the mental image I'd been nurturing of a therapeutic stroll up to it in the sunshine was completely obliterated. The thought of getting out of this foul wind and into the warm atmosphere of the pub opposite was irresistible. What, on a day like this, could be more appealing than a pint and a large plate of steaming Shepherds pie!

An hour later, having consumed two pints and satiated my hunger with my favourite dish, tiredness took over. As much as I tried to fight it, my heavy eyelids couldn't support themselves; every few minutes my head would drop causing me to come to with a start. Even the sight of the barmaid's ample appendages, which were fighting to release themselves from her skimpy top, couldn't keep me awake. With a massive effort I lifted myself out of the chair, shouted my goodbye's over towards the bar (which nobody heard of course) and walked out into the biting wind.

Climbing the ten flights of stairs up to my room depleted the last vestiges of energy that I could muster. Having decided now to give up the fight, I locked the door, got undressed and crawled into bed.

At seven o'clock a loud bang aroused me from my dreams. I sat up trying to work out what it could have been, and then realized it was Stubbs slamming his door shut on his way down to the dining room. I sprung out of bed, crept over to the door and listened. Yes, I could hear him descending the last few flights of stairs. It would now be safe to use the bathroom . . . have a quick wash and prepare myself for the evening with Clive and Rachel. If I left before seven thirty, Stubbs would still be in the dining room which would rule out any chance of bumping into him on the staircase.

With lightening speed, within ten minutes, I'd washed, changed and was standing at the bar about to order my first pint, when I received a hefty slap across the shoulders.

"Tom, my old friend, what are you having?" Benson enquired.

"Oh I'm just waiting for some friends, a pint of best I guess."

"Nice to know you've got friends, very useful people to have eh? Ha-ha."

I was quite determined this time to drink at my own slow pace rather than compete with a camel.

"Not going back for dinner tonight then?"

"No, we're going off to eat somewhere later; a curry I think."

"Ooh that sounds good to me. You can't beat a nice hot Vindaloo on a night like this; warms the old cockles a bit eh? Mind you, I bet she could do that for you as well Ha-ha," he said looking at the barmaid.

"Yes indeed," I said, finding the subtle cut and thrust of Benson's repartee slightly wanting.

"Have you spoken to our new resident yet?"

"No, I don't think so, who's that . . . which resident?"

"Gawd, which planet do you young people live on eh? There's only one new one as far as I know, 'Vince', Vincent Stubbs. He's a bit of a strange fellow, very tense if you know what I mean. . . . He's a photographer apparently. Said he might pop over here later; I told him this pub's got certain attractions, he-he," he said, giving the barmaid a sickening licentious leer.

Much to my relief, a windswept Clive and Rachel walked into the bar and interrupted the 'conversation'. I introduced Benson and bought a round of drinks. The three of us then retreated to a table nearby.

"How long have you been in here?" Clive asked me.

"Only ten minutes or so."

"Yes, don't lie to us Tom," Rachel said laughing, "now we know now how you spend your time. There's something about 'writers'. . . I think they were all born in pubs."

The banter between us continued for a while until Benson re-appeared.

"Excuse me, sorry to interrupt; I just wanted Tom to say hello to Vince, our new resident."

I froze. I'd been sitting with my back to the door, and hadn't noticed Stubbs enter the pub.

"Vince," he shouted over to the bar, "come over and say hello to Tom. I don't think you two have spoken yet."

Slowly, the menacing figure of Stubbs walked over to where I was sitting. He fixed an icy stare on me and smirked.

"Another drink for you all perhaps?" he said.

"Er . . . no thanks," I said, trying with immense difficulty to maintain an even tone to my voice. "We're just leaving."

"That's a pity," Stubbs replied, "I'm sure we'd have found a lot to talk about. But don't worry," he said staring at me, "you and I don't exactly live far from each other do we? I feel sure that we'll get on . . . like a . . . like a house on fire."

Chapter 4

"Are you alright Tom?" Rachel asked me as Clive studied the menu at the Golden Tandoori.

"You went as white as a ghost, and you were shaking, when that chap came over to us in the pub. . .Vance was it, or Vince, I think he said his name was."

"Yes I noticed that," Clive agreed. "Something about him; something quite sinister I thought."

"Creepy if you ask me," Rachel conferred.

"No, I'm fine," I said unconvincingly. "I didn't sleep very well last night, I was thinking about the book. Its building up to a fairly crucial point . . . it requires a lot of thought and concentration. Sometimes it gets difficult to switch off."

"Christ, I'm pleased I'm not a writer. I'd hate to end up in the state you're in; you look absolutely knackered," Clive commented giving me a knowing grin.

"You won't be saying that when I'm sitting in my country house with the new Porsche sitting in the driveway. Interesting though, I had in fact seen Vince, or Mr Stubbs, as my landlady calls him, a couple of times in the dining room in the building where I'm staying. I thought he looked a bit menacing then . . . I"

"A bit menacing," Rachel interrupted as she snapped a poppadom into numerous pieces sending them flying all over the table, "I think that's the biggest understatement I've heard in a long time: he looks positively evil."

"Well now that we are here, does anyone fancy a curry?" Clive asked sardonically.

I was relieved, when after the third time of being asked if we were ready to order, Rachel had at last settled on a vegetable curry.   Clive and I knew exactly what we wanted before we'd got anyway near the restaurant. We would though, have been quite content to sit there for an hour or so drinking pints of draught Cobra, but it was doubtful that the waiter would have been that accommodating. The last time we tried this, we were told in no uncertain terms that this was a restaurant and not a pub. Although the proprietor was flattered that we enjoyed the subtle flavour of Indian beer; we were nonetheless expected to order food at the same time.

"How is the estate agency business going at the moment, are you selling many properties?" I asked Clive.

"Well it's sort of teetering along. Business isn't particularly brisk. I suppose we're moving enough houses to pay the overheads. The problems as always are the chains. The number of sales that fall through seem to be increasing . . . but oh . . . it's a job I suppose. Have to be thankful for that I guess when you consider the number of people that are unemployed at the moment."

"Have you still got that shady mortgage broker working with you?" I asked.

"You mean Duncan . . . Duncan Brown; yes of course . . . without him we wouldn't sell anything. He's not really shady as you call him; he just bends the rules a bit. If he didn't incorporate a little creativity in the applications, people wouldn't stand a chance. If everyone stuck strictly to the rules I think the whole thing would come to a standstill."

"Yes I suppose there's some truth in that." I said. "Thinking about it, there aren't many areas of business or commerce that are uncontaminated. No one is going to run a business for altruistic reasons. Estate agents are hardly going to lose any sleep if the people they've sold a house to cant find the mortgage repayments. All they're worried about is getting their commission."

"Precisely, hard as it may sound that's the undeniable truth." Clive agreed.

"Take the game you were in for example, Clive began: your main concern . . . not yours personally, but the company you worked for; was to extract premiums off people in the hope that the risk covered by the insurance never materializes. When it did, they'd fight tooth and nail using every trick in the book, to avoid paying out. Bad losers, I think you'd call them. I know this is true from the few claims that I've made. Yes I agree with you; it's all totally corrupt and immoral. In fact if they put interest rates up again, I think I'll join you and become a writer. "

I was now regretting we'd got on this subject. Clive's comment was a poignant reminder of exactly what Stubbs had expressed the previous evening.

"Are you really alright Tom?" Rachel asked me again, "Sorry to keep asking, but you've gone very white again."

"Yes, don't worry, I'm fine. I was just thinking about the past. When I think back on it, I can't understand why I did it for so long . . . Insurance I mean. Although one good thing has come out of it though . . . it's given me an idea for my next book."

"What's that?" Rachel asked. "Or aren't we allowed to know."

"Yes of course, I had this idea that the protagonist; somebody like me for example, was working for an insurance company, doing the job I was doing; and finds a reason not to pay out on a big claim. You know . . . some petty technical get out clause in the policy . . . and."

"You mean a memoir." Rachel interrupted.

"No, its fiction . . . where was I? Oh yes, I had this idea that maybe it was a factory, something like this, that got destroyed in a fire or a flood, with the owner losing everything, and then, perhaps a few years later, carrying out a personal vendetta against the insurance company manager who'd declined the claim. I thought about this man brooding over the injustice, becoming obsessed with the notion that his life was now ruined, and was determined to wreak vengeance against the protagonist."

"It sounds like a good plot," Clive said, "a bit far fetched though don't you think? I mean in real life people don't carry on like that do they? I'm sure a lot of people feel like taking some serious pro-active measures in these situations; but you never actually hear about anyone doing it."

"Yes, that's true," Rachel agreed. "Mind you if you did write it and if it was successful and made into a film; that man, 'Vance, or Vince was it? That creepy man we saw in the pub would be an excellent person to star as the factory owner. He's just as I would imagine somebody like that to be."

"I'll have to work on it," I said looking down at the chicken madras that just arrived. How's the travel business going?" I asked Rachel.

"Oh it's boring really. People think there's something romantic and exciting about arranging all these foreign trips for high powered business executives. But in truth they tend to be a complete pain in the arse. Always going on about what they want in their hotels. You can quickly work out which ones have ever done any serious travelling, and the ones that have always been molly coddled and start complaining if the shower is one degree out, or if the mini bar hasn't got the particular brand of water they like in it. I'm seriously thinking about going back to secretarial work. The solicitors Julia works for are going to be looking for someone soon, and I'm tempted to apply."

I desperately wanted to confide in them; to have someone to talk to. I deeply regretted mentioning the book scenario. I'd been toying with danger. I knew I couldn't . . . I mustn't speak to them about Stubbs . . . the terrifying ordeal I'd gone through just twenty four hours ago. They would have insisted that I go to the police. That's the way people thought. They would have meant well, but that's as far as it goes. Had they of been at the receiving end of Stubbs's violent tirade, they might just have had some inkling of the predicament I faced. Trying to explain to them that I also felt anger and disgust at my own actions five years ago; and genuine sympathy for the unjust way Stubbs had been treated would have gone over their heads. No, I was an outsider; no one could possibly comprehend my emotions. If I'd been foolish enough to tell them that I'd agreed to give away the money for my book, assuming of course that there would be any money, they would have immediately assumed that I was mentally ill.

The more I thought about this, the more detached and alienated I felt. I'd enjoyed seeing them, but now I couldn't wait to get away. We stood outside the restaurant for a few minutes vowing not to leave it so long before we met up again; said our goodbyes, then I started walking slowly back in the freezing cold drizzle to Albion Mansions.

Several burning questions were tormenting me. Stubbs had mentioned weekly progress reports. Did this mean that I would be subject to further ferocious beatings every week, if the work I'd produced didn't meet with his expectations? Was I going to have to endure further violent verbal abuse regardless of whatever efforts I'd made? And what if at the end of the two month period Stubbs had agreed; the finished work was rejected? It was hard to imagine him adopting a conciliatory or sympathetic stance. Trying to picture him saying 'Oh well Tom; you've tried your best. It was kind of you to offer me the money from your book, but we have to be philosophical about these things'. No, this wouldn't happen. Having waited and contained his anger he would be like an unexploded bomb. All hell would break loose. He was quite emphatic about another thing: he said he wanted to see any correspondence sent or received. Somehow this would have to be circumvented. Perhaps I could phone my agent and say I'd moved . . . give them a change of address. That way I'd know the outcome before he did, which would give me time to escape without having to break the news to him. Yes, of course, that would be wise; a well thought out plan; but whose address could I use without too many questions being asked? Another way would be to phone them . . . my agents . . . and explain that I didn't have a fixed abode when the finished work was submitted and that I would phone them at regular intervals . . . yes this could be another possibility.

If the worse thing happened and the script *was* rejected; what would I do then? I needed to have a contingency plan. Moving out of Albion Mansions and hiding somewhere wouldn't offer much peace of mind. He'd somehow tracked me down on this occasion and he would definitely do so again. If I did this and he caught up with me, he'd beat me to a pulp.   The man was obsessively deranged; he had nothing else to do with his time. He was consumed with bitterness and hatred. Another way would be a change of identity, or move out of the country. The trouble though with these ideas, apart from being extreme; was they both required money which I wouldn't have. My brain was buzzing as I crept up the stairs to my room trying to remember to avoid the ones that creaked. Yes, yes, yes; something had to be thought up . . . and soon. The nearer I became to completing the book, the worse it would become. I'd be a complete nervous wreck; I probably wouldn't even be able to think when it got to the last few weeks, apart from attempting to write anything worthwhile.

It was now just before midnight. I slowly and carefully put my key into the lock opened the door and tiptoed inside my room. No sign or sound of him thank God, I thought, as I closed the door and drew the bolt across it.

'Oh blast, bugger it', I muttered to myself, 'I forgot to use the toilet on the way up'. I pressed my ear to the door for a couple of minutes and couldn't hear a sound. 'He must be asleep', I convinced myself, and crept out again to relieve the course of nature. 'Bloody beer', I muttered again, got undressed and fell upon my unmade single bed.

A few hours later I awoke with a start. A lot of bangs, thuds, thumps and voices; somebody talking in the room next door . . . an argument. At first I thought I was dreaming, but no, this noise was coming from the room Stubbs occupied. I sat bolt upright in bed trying to make out what was being said. I urgently needed to release some more beer, I started berating myself: 'Why the hell did I drink so much, bloody fool, stupid, stupid thing to do!' I got up, the room was freezing. Shivering with the cold I pressed my ear against the door and listened. Only the voice of Stubbs could be heard. 'I won't wait' it said, 'I'll fucking kill the little piece of shit now' . . . bang . . . 'yes, that's what I'll do, I'll go in there and punch his fucking lights out', another loud thud followed, and the dividing wall between our two rooms shook. My heart dropped, I realized he must have been thumping the wall with his fists, and as he shouted with mounting anger. Whatever had happened to him earlier in the evening had driven him over the edge into a violent uncontrollable frenzy.

I was busting to use the toilet, but was too terrified to open the door. I looked around the room for a receptacle of some kind . . . anything . . . I couldn't wait much longer. 'Oh God, what can I do'? I said to myself. At last deciding I just couldn't wait any longer; I opened the window, an icy blast filled the room; I stood on a chair and peed freely out into the street five floors below.

For a further forty five minutes I lay in a foetal position in bed with a pillow over my head trying to pretend that it wasn't happening. Finally around four o'clock the noise died down and I must have drifted off to sleep. At seven fifteen the loose pane of glass vibrating aroused me from my slumbers. Exhausted and frightened, I got out of bed, crept over to the door and pressed my tired ear against it. All was quiet. Stealthily I opened the door and made my way across the hall to the bathroom. This morning I was in luck; the water was hot allowing me to slowly come to life. Pressing my ear against the bathroom door, I carefully chose my moment, and tiptoed back to my room and bolted the door.

My mind was racing; I couldn't seem to concentrate on a single thought pattern. Everything was an unanswered question. What could have caused him to exhibit this violent outburst? Was it a reaction to seeing me enjoying myself with friends earlier in the evening? Could it have been due to my refusal to accept a round of drinks that he'd had offered to buy? How often were these violent tirades going to occur now? Was he now becoming even *more* dangerous . . . even murderous?

The more I thought about it and the more I questioned, the more terrified I became. Comparing myself to a frightened hunted animal, I wondered if I was on the verge of a nervous breakdown. What seemed to be a mild headache when I woke up was now a searing throbbing pain making me feel dizzy and nauseous. With a supreme effort, and now trembling from both fear and tiredness, I warily made my way down to the dining room.

As I walked through the doors I sensed all was not well.

"It's probably a leaking overflow pipe," Jack said with a certain air of authority as he dragged an enormous ladder through the dining room.

"Yes dear, you're right most of the time; I expect that's what it is. There's always *something* with an old property like this. I don't know where we'd be without you." Mrs Hoskins declared scurrying back into the kitchen.

I quickly considered that Jack's instant diagnosis was indeed quite logical; after all what else could explain a gush of water running down the front of a building at three o'clock in the morning? Unfortunately in my desperation to relieve myself, I'd forgotten that Mrs Hoskins slept in the ground floor front room. Steaming hot urine cascading down five floors and hitting the pavement just outside her bedroom window must have sounded like a waterfall. The fact that Jack would undoubtedly be engaged for the rest of the morning trying to trace 'the fault' was in my eyes fully justified. I owed him one for fusing the lights which had ultimately led to the loss of my manuscript. Mrs Hoskins wasn't exactly blameless either; she'd chosen to let the room next to me to a raving psychopath who had beaten me up and was more than likely going to kill me. No, I shouldn't feel guilty; the stupid woman had got away lightly.

All the regulars were firmly ensconced at their respective tables. What a sad and depressing example of life's failures they collectively represented. The flotsam and jetsam of hopelessly dejected and broken spirits. Each one of them desperately clinging on to their last few tattered strands of pride and dignity. All trying in their own way to 'keep their end up' . . . 'maintain some sort of standard'. . '.not let the side down etc'.

Eric Bottomly was for some reason uncharacteristically effusive, even enquiring as to how my writing was progressing. This morning he seemed to bear a striking likeness to some sort of amphibious reptile. It definitely was his pointed weasel face and scraggy neck that did it. Roy Benson was clearly hung-over; his face was a strange and unhealthy puce colour with eyes to match. He just managed to lift his head a couple of inches away from his newspaper and utter a muffled 'good morning' and that was it.

Much to my relief, there was no sign of Stubbs. I wondered if he and Benson had stayed in the pub for the rest of the evening. If Stubbs was in a similar condition to Benson it would have been possible that he too was suffering a serious indisposition. In the end my curiosity got the better of me, I had to ask Benson.

"Did you have a good evening?" I enquired timidly.

Benson's head was obviously very sore. It took him a few seconds to lift it up a few degrees and then turn it slowly in my direction.

"Yes . . . I suspect we might *just* have outstayed our welcome though," he replied.

"Why, what time did you leave?"

"Ooh, you don't ask a man a question like that," he replied, "it's a bit like asking a woman her age!"

"I understand," I replied. I didn't really need an answer; the stale alcohol fumes emanating from him filled the dining room.

"How about you, did you have a good evening?"

"Yes thank you," I said.

"A bit upset he was last night . . . you know . . . Vince," he whispered confidently, leaning across the table. "Didn't really understand why it was. After you left with your friends he seemed to get very agitated . . . started swearing a lot . . . couldn't really understand it to be honest; I think he's still getting over the loss of his wife . . . poor chap. Now if it had of been my wife I'd have been celebrating eh? Ha-ha."

"Yes, quite so." I replied. "Was there any trouble then?"

"Well not exactly trouble . . . no . . . I wouldn't say that. I wouldn't like to fall out with him though, let's put it that way. I'm sure he's a nice enough chap . . . it's just . . . I can't really put my finger on it . . . he's very tense, I think he finds it hard to relax if you know what I mean."

"Yes, I think I understand," I replied. It was becoming increasingly evident that the fragile agreement I'd made with Stubbs was in jeopardy. Stubbs was clearly far more unstable and disturbed than

I'd realized. Benson after all, was a simple pleasant enough fellow and if he had serious reservations after a few hours in the pub, then I needed to be concerned. After the manic violent outburst at three o'clock this morning, I now realized that Stubbs was on a precipice; He could very easily lose control and carry out a murderous attack at the slightest provocation. The prospect of me continuing to write under this black cloud of intimidation was becoming even more improbable. Something had to be done, and quickly. Trying to bury my head in the sand might have worked, but not now, with Stubbs behaving like this.

I wolfed down my breakfast and cautiously made my way back to my room, went inside and locked the door. A plan . . . that's what I need I said to myself . . . some kind of plan. Must move out of here . . . can't go on like this . . . definitely not . . . quite impossible. After an hour of sitting by my typewriter smoking and going through the same arguments, I ended up where I'd started. Perhaps the most logical way to resolve this would be for me to approach Stubbs and tactfully try and reason with him. If he understood that my intentions really were genuine and honourable, he might listen. All I had to get across was that with the best will in the world, I just couldn't write under these circumstances. The money from any advance I might get, he could have; not only that, I'd be pleased to give it to him; I'd explained this to him before. But he must allow me to finish the book in peace for this to happen. Yes, I thought, this would be a sound move. With any luck he'd realize that I really was sincere, and was trying to offer some recompense.

After a further hour of deliberation, I decided to take my chances and put this plan into action. With every hope of this strategy working, I walked out of my room and knocked gently on the adjoining door. Having done so, I was overcome with fear, I wanted to run but felt rooted to the spot. 'Must do it' I said to myself and knocked again more loudly. I heard some movement from inside the room; suddenly the door opened. Stubbs appeared unshaven and bare footed with an old Paisley dressing gown wrapped around him. He poked his head around the door and looked along the landing. His eyes then focused on me. "What can I do for you?" he enquired menacingly.

"I wondered if we might have a word." I asked in my practiced macho voice.

"I don't see why not," he replied, "come in."
I entered the room with extreme caution. My heart was pounding making it difficult for me to catch my breath. The room stank of stale alcohol and even staler sweat.

"Now what is it you want a word about," he said encroaching into my personal space with his face scowling and only a foot away from mine.

"Can we sit down?" I asked, reeling from the stench of his breath, hoping to put a little more distance between us.
He picked up some clothing from one of the chairs and threw them across the room onto the bed. "There's a chair . . . sit on it," he demanded.

"Thank you . . . The thing is . . . we haven't spoken since our first unfortunate encounter, and I fully understand that your emotions were shall we say . . . rife. I don't want to go over old ground, I . . ."

"Look, say what you've got to say you little shit and then piss off. I'm not in the mood to listen to a load of verbal garbage."

"I'm trying . . . trying to explain something."

"Well fucking try harder. Come to the point you little rat before I lose my temper."

"Look to put it as briefly as I can: I want you to have the money from my book . . . the point is though, you must allow me to write it. I can't write if you keep threatening me."

"Threatening you . . . Threatening you? What the hell are you talking about?"

"I think you must know what I'm talking about . . .last night . . .or this morning, early this morning; you were hitting the wall between us . . .you were shouting . . .something about 'punching my fucking lights out'. I can't write like this; I can't sleep, I can't think; without sleep, I just can't function. I want to finish the book; I want you to have the money from it . . . but . . . but you've got to understand what I'm saying."

He stared at me for a few moments, and then looking down at the floor took a couple of steps towards me. "Got to understand have I?"

"All I mean is that . . ."

"What I *do* understand, is that you, you nasty little creep, have ruined my life. You're now telling me I've got to understand that I mustn't interfere with your beauty sleep. You spend an enjoyable evening out with your friends, come back here tired and couldn't sleep; and you're now telling me I've disturbed you precious sleeping pattern. Ha, that's fucking rich."

The veins pulsating in his head were about to burst. I knew that it didn't take much provocation for him to completely lose control. He was now dangerously close to it. Nonetheless I had to seize this opportunity: try and reach some sort of compromise, this might be my only chance.

"It's not that at all," I continued. "If I could just undo what's happened . . . the insurance . . . I mean; I would. If I had money, I would happily give it to you. I've already said that I'm sorry. The only way I can offer any proof of my sincere intention to put things right between us, is to come up with the offer I have. If that's not going to placate you at least in some way, then there's nothing more I can do. If the anger you feel can't be contained you might as well kill me now; because I'm not going to finish the book unless I can have the peace to do so. I'm sorry, but that's really all I wanted to say."

He paused for a moment obviously taken aback by this outburst. He walked away from me and seemed to be staring out of the window. Paralysed with fear and visibly trembling, with the words I'd just uttered ringing through my head, I waited for the violent onslaught which I was convinced he was about to unleash.

During these seconds that seemed like hours, I was bitterly regretting my actions. I'd badly misjudged the situation. I was trying to get a raving madman to see reason. I suspected now that this was probably the biggest mistake I'd ever made in my life.

After a minute or so he turned towards me and stared as if contemplating his next move. "Are you intimating by any chance that you'd prefer that I left you alone until the book is finished?"

"In a word . . . yes."

"If I agree to this, how will I know that you're honouring your agreement with me?"

"You just have to trust me."

"Do I now? I have to trust *you* after you've ruined my life. That's the funniest thing I've ever heard."

"It's not meant to be funny . . . I'm quite serious. I'm asking you to leave me alone, to allow me to finish the book without any meetings or contact between us. Call it a deal if you like."

"Okay, you've got yourself a deal, you nasty little shit. I shall still be keeping a close eye on you though. If you've got any ideas of moving out of here . . . running away . . . I would forget it. If you attempt anything like that I'll find you and I'll fucking kill you. Is that absolutely clear?"

"Yes, it couldn't be any clearer." I replied. I then held my hand out to shake hands with him.

"You've got the concession you wanted: Now fuck off and get out of my sight," he replied, making no attempt to offer his hand.

"Thank you," I said, unable to express the relief I felt at not only escaping what might have resulted in a murderous attack, but having been able to reach some sort of agreement with this man.

The unexpected outcome of these perilous negotiations made me feel more positive. The relative peace of mind I felt, engendered a renewed burst of enthusiasm. For the rest of the day I sat in front of my typewriter hitting the keys for all I was worth. By seven o'clock I'd contributed a further two thousand words towards my goal; the most productive days writing since

I started. I congratulated myself on having the courage to confront him. Although it was a nerve racking experience, it had done the trick. Stubbs now had to realize that he couldn't just push people around . . . threaten them and attack them . . . it didn't work. No . . . anyone who thought Tom Dunford could be pushed around and intimidated was seriously mistaken!

Apart from a few awkward encounters in the dining room, and the occasional meeting on the staircase; I was able to continue as before without the unnecessary pressure from Stubbs. The most pressing problem I had to contend with right now was getting in and out of my room to use the bathroom. Both my ears had become extremely red and sore from pressing them against the door of my room, checking to see if the coast was clear. A ready solution to this problem appeared completely out of the blue when I came across an old stethoscope in a junk shop. Not only was it less painful on my ears; it was so much easier to hear through it.

As the days and weeks went by, it soon came to the point when the book was finished; and two weeks ahead of schedule. 'At last . . . finally cracked it', I said to myself, my heart nearly exploding with joy and ecstasy. Without doubt this called for a small celebration. Perhaps a precursory few drinks with Clive would be a good idea. We could then arrange to go and eat somewhere another evening. In order to avoid any possibility of bumping into Stubbs; I suggested that we meet in the Bulls Head, a small friendly pub in the town centre.

"So what's next?" Clive asked before taking a long swig of best bitter.

"Well, there's some distance to go," I replied, it's a case now of sending it off and keeping everything crossed . . . just hoping that they like it."

"And what if they don't?"

"Oh, that's probably the hardest part . . . coping with rejection; after all the effort that's gone into it. They seemed quite enthusiastic about the first three chapters, so unless there's something radically wrong with it . . ."

"Yeah, I suppose it's just like me selling six houses and then at the eleventh hour finding the whole thing collapse like a house of cards."

"How's Julia, do you or Rachel see much of her now?" I asked.

"Yes, funny you should mention Julia. She and Rachel were having lunch the other day in that tea shop place 'The Copper Kettle'; you know that place in the high street; when that bloke Vince walked in. Rachel was saying he sat at a table right next to them which seemed a bit strange: there were lots of other free tables: anyway he kept staring at them and Rachel recognised him."

"Good God," I said without thinking, "what happened?"

"Well nothing actually happened except that according to Rachel, he got up when they were about to leave and spoke to them . . . well, to Rachel at first."

"What did he say?"

"Hang on, let me try and remember . . . ah yes, apparently he mentioned something about that evening when we were all in the Crown and Anchor together. Said he remembered her face and was trying to remember her name. That seemed strange enough to

Rachel; but then he looked at Julia . . . yes . . . that was the weird thing . . . he just said 'you must be Julia', before she could reply, he said 'I'm a friend of Tom's; he's told me a lot about you', and that, they both thought, was quite bizarre . . . well so do I really."

The sense of euphoria I had been feeling suddenly evaporated. A cold chill ran down my spine. What was Stubbs up to? Everything seemed under control, this was an unforeseen and sinister development. The two women thought his behaviour was strange and justifiably so. I must have gone quiet.

"Are you alright Tom?" Clive asked. "You seem to be lost in thought."

"No, I'm fine. Is Julia . . . is Julia with anyone at the moment?"

"No, not as far as we know. I think she's been out with a few people, but nothing serious. Why have you got something in mind?"

"Well, I was just wondering if it would be a good idea for the four of us to get together, I was thinking tomorrow night . . .have a decent meal out . . .you know; a proper celebration."

"Yes, that sounds like a great idea. Hang on I'll go and phone Rachel and get her to give Julia a ring to find out if she's free tomorrow night. I'll get Rachel to give us a ring back here in the pub once they've spoken together; Gives us an excuse to get another couple of pints in!"

As Clive was waiting to get change for the payphone, my brain was racing. It occurred to me that Julia might now be in some sort of danger. Was Stubbs planning to do something to Julia if my book was rejected? Was this what it was all about? Perhaps I ought to come clean with her . . . explain what had been going on; after all *she* had a right to know if somebody was about to do her some harm . . . particularly a raving madman like Stubbs. The problem is that knowing Julia, the first thing she'd want to do is go to the police. This would then put not just her, but me, in imminent danger . . . no that's an understatement . . . Stubbs would kill me, or disable me for life.

"All done," Clive said as he placed another two pints on the table. Rachel is going to call us back when she's had a word with Julia. Where do you fancy going? There's a new Italian restaurant farther up the road; evidently the food in there is first class."

"Yup, that sounds perfect to me."

"Well if it's definitely on tomorrow, we'll drop in there when we leave here and book a table, yes?"

"Yes, good idea," I said.

A few pints later the telephone rang and Clive jumped up and answered it. His happy youthful face seemed to suddenly take on a more serious and concerned appearance. I could just hear him saying 'when', 'when was this'? The conversation lasted a further couple of minutes and he replaced the receiver.

"Not on?" I asked, as Clive returned to the table.

". . . Yes, yes . . . it's all okay for tomorrow night. Julia said she'd be delighted to join us . . . it's just . . . that man. . . .Vince . . . he was waiting on the corner outside Julia's flat when she got home from work this evening. Evidently he was sitting in an old car watching her going into her flat. This doesn't sound right at all.

Julia was asking Rachel if she should report it to the police. I think she should, don't you?"

Chapter 5

Needless to say I couldn't get to sleep after I'd returned to my room. Hunched up in my single bed with a blanket tightly wound around me; I remained wide awake, my brain buzzing; trying to make sense out of what was going on. The more I thought about it, the more confused I became. Things were now getting out of control. Julia would have been well within her rights to contact the police . . . maybe she'd done so already. If this was the case, the police could turn up at any moment and question Stubbs. Stubbs wasn't in his right mind, he was paranoid; he'd assume there was some sort of collusion between me and Julia, and that we'd conspired to get him arrested. What then? If I hadn't seen Clive this evening, I wouldn't have known anything about it. At least now if the police suddenly turned up and started interviewing him, I'd know that would be the time to make a run for it. But run where?

The more I thought about it, the woollier my thinking became. I was trying to rationalize the thinking of an insane person. Attempting to predict the thought processes of a madman was a pointless exercise. What was going through his mind was anyone's guess. He'd agree something one minute . . . then change his mind the next. Perhaps I ought to get out of here now . . . tonight, and call the police myself. But where could I go? And what about Julia? The problem was that Stubbs hadn't actually done anything yet. There was certainly no evidence to prove that he'd already viciously attacked me. The police wouldn't hold him or charge him with anything: how could they? I'd read of many cases where people in similar circumstances had complained to the police, and the police did nothing . . .nothing that is, until the person in question was released after questioning, lost control, and then carried out a frenzied attack upon their innocent victim for going to the police in the first place. Of course if he attacked Julia, then the police *would* do something . . . but it could well be too late. I couldn't wait for this to happen.

The more I kept procrastinating the worse my dilemma appeared. I was finding it difficult to breathe; my heart was thumping away. Beads of perspiration were running down my face. I got out of bed and opened the window. I stuck my head outside for a few moments and tried to take deep slow gasps of the bitterly cold night air. At first this seemed to help, but after a few moments I started shivering uncontrollably. I closed the window, dragged a blanket off the bed and wrapped it around myself.

As the minutes and hours passed, I remained in the same position racking my weary brain trying to find a way forward, some compromise, a solution. Eventually it started getting light; I threw the blanket off and crept over to the window and peered out at the street below. The orange coloured street lighting bouncing off the wet pavements created a strange and surreal image; the similarity to stage scenery was the first thought that flashed through my tired mind.

Reflecting that the whole night had passed; one of the most unpleasant nights I could remember; without having reached any resolution, made me feel weak and impotent. Perhaps if I could stay awake, something might occur to me as the day progressed. I tried to look at things more optimistically; the book was finished; all I had to do was to send it off and pray. If . . . no, think positively . . . not if . . . *when* my agent confirms that they'll represent me; I will have crossed the first hurdle. I could then inform him, which must take the heat off. He'd relax a little knowing that I meant what I said, and was being honourable. Yes, things weren't *that* bad. I was going out tonight; seeing Julia again, no, things weren't quite as bad as they seemed. Julia, although a bit scatty, was reasonably level headed; I could explain to her that although Stubbs was strange, he was quite harmless and she shouldn't worry too much. The best thing to do would be to play it down. I could then approach him and explain that the book was finished and fairly soon now I'd would know the outcome. I could tell him in no uncertain terms that if he harassed Julia any more she would go to the police and there would be nothing I could do to stop it. I'd also tell him that if he continued with this, I would rescind my agreement with him. Well . . . perhaps not go quite that far. But there *were* limits to what I would be prepared to put up with. He'd have no choice; he'd have to accept this.

A problem I still had to find a solution to was which address I should use when the completed manuscript was sent off. I decided to wait and ask Julia if I could use her address. I'd make some excuse . . . something about suspecting other residents of stealing my post . . . she would understand. This had to be done. The possibility of him, suspicious and paranoid as he was; taking any letters addressed to me couldn't be ignored.

That could have disastrous consequences. The prospect of him knowing the outcome before I did was unthinkable.

Despite a magnificent effort to stay awake, by two o'clock I'd reached the point of physical and mental exhaustion. One thing I had managed to achieve was posting the manuscript. I'd decided to use Julia's address and put a brief note in with it explaining that I'd moved. I *knew* she wouldn't mind. Now, I didn't care about anything now . . . sleep was the only thing that mattered. Within five minutes I was dead to the world.

At seven o'clock I awoke with a start, hearing Stubbs's door bang as he left for the dining room. A perfect opportunity I thought to use the bathroom time to have a quick wash before meeting the others in the restaurant at eight.

A few hours sleep and a splash in cold water had made a world of difference, I now felt alive again and even excited at the prospect of the imminent celebration.

Ambling towards the Tavernetta in the damp November air, I was in good spirits. No longer feeling like an impoverished writer emerging from a seedy attic room, I felt like a successful author. A quick glance at my elegant reflection in the plate glass window of the Kentucky fried chicken take-away reinforced this notion. Tonight, dressed in a smart sports jacket with a collar and tie, I was something. People would soon be stopping me in the street asking for my autograph. 'Aren't you the man that wrote 'One Murder Too Many'? They would say reverentially, 'Oh I did enjoy that', 'when is your next book due out', etc. Oh yes, things were looking up at last!

The restaurant was virtually empty when I arrived. An unctuous 'Italian' waiter with a strong Manchurian accent greeted me effusively and showed me to the 'reserved' table. I ordered a jug of red house wine and in my excitement managed to drink three glasses of it before the others arrived. The first glass had a flavour not dissimilar to battery acid, but my palate had adjusted sufficiently by the time I'd swallowed the third glass.

I couldn't see the others arrive as my chair was facing away from the window. I did hear them though. Julia's husky laugh preceded her by at least two minutes as they walked along the street approaching the restaurant. The waiters obviously heard it too, which was patently apparent by their body language. They both appeared to have received some form of electrical charge on hearing the approaching customers; now they were psyched up, and ready for this evenings onslaught.

A further jug of house wine appeared and the four of us chattered away for twenty minutes or so. As the restaurant filled up with more and more people the general cacophony became deafening. To add to this, the waiters chose to sing parts of old Italian cavatinas as loud as they could in between taking orders. A third one who appeared from nowhere, (perhaps he came in late) decided to add something to the frenetic atmosphere by shouting out something incomprehensible in Spanish or Portuguese and ringing a bell. I was beginning to wonder if the somnolent hypnotic sitar music of The Golden Tandoori mightn't have been a better alternative, at least we could have heard one another and would have been able to have had a sensible conversation.

At least the food was good. Garlic mushrooms, calamari, and veal in a cream sauce with tiny roast potatoes, made a pleasant change from Mrs Hoskins spaghetti bolognaise which I was mercifully saved from this evening. The conversation didn't get around to Stubbs and the fact that he'd been lurking around Julia's flat until much later in the evening.

"Have you seen any more of him?" Clive asked Julia.

"No thank God I haven't. I was just saying to Rachel on the way here that if I see him again, I'm going straight to the police. It's not good for the nerves, every time I come and go from the flat I'm now expecting to see him; it's horrible."

"How many times have you seen him . . . I mean hanging around outside?" I asked.

"Twice," Julia replied. "The last time was last night, he was sitting in his car watching me go into the flat, and the time before that . . . about three days before that, he was standing on the corner looking up at all the buildings, or that's what it seemed like. When I was inside I peeked through the curtains and watched him. He was staring directly at my flat . . . he stayed there for another twenty minutes or so and then walked off. And then a couple of days later he followed Rachel and me into the 'Copper Kettle'. He said hello to Rachel and said he recognised her from an evening when the three of you were together, which was vaguely plausible. But he knew my name which was spooky. He homed in on me with those piercing blue eyes of his and said 'you must be Julia', how the hell would he know that? "

"I don't know. I really don't know what it's all about," I said, "but don't worry Julia, I'll have a word with him tomorrow and try and find out what he's playing at. He *is* a strange fellow I agree, but he's pretty harmless. You probably remember how worried I was when he seemed to be following me: but now I realize he's just lonely."

"Hmm, anyone that lonely has got serious problems, I would think," she said unconvinced by my assessment.

As the evening drew to a close; Clive and Rachel said their goodbyes and jumped into a taxi. Julia and I continued talking outside the restaurant; mainly about my book. Julia couldn't seem to get off the subject of Stubbs.

"Do you promise you'll speak to him tomorrow?" she asked.
"Yes of course I will, don't worry."

"But that's precisely *it* . . . I am worried. To be honest Tom I'm scared to go back to my flat now in case he's hanging around outside. It's alright for you, you're a man, you can defend yourself."
I smiled wryly. If only she knew that I was as terrified and defenceless as she was against this violent lunatic.

"Well how about if I walk back with you and see you in, would that make you feel any easier?"

"Oh yes it would, but it's not fair, it's taking you a couple of miles out of your way. Perhaps we could get a taxi?"

"No, that's fine; let's walk; we can chat on the way."
The mist had now cleared, the temperature had risen a few degrees, or perhaps it was the considerable amount

of alcohol we'd consumed that made us impervious to the cold. We walked along holding hands, laughing and chatting as if we'd always been together. When at last we were outside Julia's flat, the conversation between us became stilted and seemed to dry up. Julia was noticeably nervous as we scoured up and down the road looking into parked cars for any sign of Stubbs. After a thorough search which revealed no unpleasant surprises, I kissed her on the cheek and promised to phone her tomorrow after I'd spoken to him.

"Won't you come in for a coffee?" she said.

"Well if you're sure I won't be keeping you up."

"Don't be silly, of course you're keeping me up, but I wouldn't suggest it if I was desperate to get to bed."

The following morning I could distinctly hear traffic outside and being now conditioned to the loose pane of glass vibrating in my window tried to work out where I was, and what had happened; with my head thumping and eyes stinging; I turned over and saw Julia's blonde head on the pillow next to me deep in sleep. Now I remembered!

For a few moments I lay there pondering my next move. What had happened between us wasn't premeditated it had just happened. Did this now mean the start of a new beginning or were Julia and I going to be back where we'd started? Perhaps it would be better not to speculate. The first thing I had to do was confront Stubbs. I'd promised her this, and this was the very reason why I was now lying here beside her.

Julia slowly adjusted her position, released a mournful sigh and opened her eyes. I laughed realizing it wasn't just me that had a pounding headache.

"Oh God," she moaned in her husky voice, "What the hell did they put in that wine?"

"Got a headache by any chance?"

"No not a headache, I feel like I've just undergone a frontal lobotomy, oh bloody hell."

"Everything has a price, don't worry; it'll wear off in about three days time."

"What's the time, oh hell, I'm going to be late for work. Could you be a star and make some coffee, I'm just going to have a quick shower, and then I'll have to run," she said, gently easing herself out of bed.

As I got the coffee underway I had a strange feeling of claustrophobia, of been trapped. I'd been here once before. Back into the spiders web once again. But hang on: Julia hadn't planned this . . . it just happened I kept telling himself. Perhaps it was just fate. Perhaps we were always meant to be together. I knew now that my life was about to take a different direction; not along the same old well trodden paths, I hoped. It would be quite pointless; it came to nothing then and it would do again. Nice as she was, Julia was a powerful personality and extremely manipulative. Had she had been willing to compromise we'd never have separated. Did she accept this? I wondered. Perhaps the six months we'd been apart had allowed her enough time to reflect.

I placed the two mugs of coffee on the table in the lounge, lighted a cigarette, and automatically walked over to the window and peered out. I knew really that Stubbs wouldn't be around at this time in the morning; he'd be sitting in the dining room at Albion Mansions. Hating to admit it, I was becoming as insecure as Julia. Today would be the day of reckoning though . . . no more pretending . . . no more fobbing it off: as soon as Julia had left I'd go straight back there and confront him once more. This time I'd get my point across in no uncertain terms. I wouldn't mince my words. No more pussy footing. What the hell did he think he was doing? No one in their right mind would put up with this. I'd made a deal with him; if he couldn't honour it then he could go and whistle for the money. He wouldn't get a penny from the book and furthermore, Julia and I would go straight to the police if he didn't behave himself. Oh yes. I've tried to be decent honest and fair; and if this is the way he's going to respond, well that's it, I said to myself.

"I must rush," Julia said as she ran out of the bathroom looking none the worse for wear. She swilled the lukewarm coffee down in one go, took a drag of my cigarette, gave me a nicotine flavoured kiss and hurried out of the door.

"Pop round this evening if you can . . . let me know how you get on with Mr Stubbs," she said before slamming the flat door. "If you like I'll cook something for us . . . yes?"

"Okay," I shouted back, "see you this evening."

The net was closing in. I'd accepted the bait and that was me done for. Julia hadn't planned this . . . of course she hadn't . . . but given the slightest opportunity she was going to capitalize on it. Why couldn't I phone her this evening? Why did it have to be a 'casual' pop round and I'll cook something? Julia wasn't silly; she had that natural female trait of being able to pull in a catch at the faintest movement on the line. They all had it. By the time you realized what had been happening; or for that matter even before then; it was often too late: you were caught . . . well and truly hitched.

It was more like an early spring morning rather than mid January; a cloudless deep blue sky, and for once, no wind. I was rehearsing my authoritative speech to Stubbs as I sauntered back to my room. I gazed into the faces of passers by as the roads leading to the town became busier; weaving in between people became something of an agility test. What would they think about my current dilemma? Had any of them ever found themselves in similar positions? Not just with people like Stubbs; but with this wretched insidious net closing in on me. Chances are they hadn't. Most of them looked far too vacuous to have ever even thought about such things, I concluded.

The first thing to do I decided as I entered Albion Mansions was to locate Mrs Hoskins. I must tell her that I wouldn't be around for dinner this evening. Then I'd go straight upstairs and approach him. The first part was easy . . . now for the second part, I said to myself whilst climbing the stairs up to my tormentor.

I checked my watch it was nine fifteen. As I tapped gently on his door, part of me was hoping that he'd had breakfast and had gone out somewhere. I couldn't hear any movement from the other side of the door so I took a deep breath and knocked again more determinedly. Suddenly the door opened. He appeared from the other side of it dressed in a pinstriped suit and the familiar black Crombie overcoat.

"Oh it's you," he said, "what is it you want?"

"I want a word with you," I said, poker faced and staring straight at him.

"Well you'd better make it quick, I'm just off out, I've got to be somewhere. Two minutes . . . say what you've got to say in two minutes and then piss off."

"That's fine with me, two minutes is *more* than enough to say what I've got to say to you."

"Come in," he said, opening the door just enough for me to squeeze through. He then closed the door and stood threateningly with his back against it. I stepped back a couple of paces attempting to put some distance between us.

"There are two things I have to tell you," I began: 'the first thing is that the book is finished; it's been sent off to my agent and as soon as I hear from them I'll let you know. The second thing is that you've been seen outside Julia's flat and I . . ."

"What are you talking about . . . been seen?"

"It's not just Julia who's seen you standing outside or sitting in your car outside her flat, it's her neighbours as well . . .there are witnesses . . .and . . ."

"Is that so?" he replied. "Now you listen to . . ."

"No . . . *you* listen to me," I said, now white as a sheet and trying to disguise the fear I felt within. Julia is all for going to the police. I've managed to dissuade her so far; I told her I'd speak to you and warn you that if it happens again, it'll be out of my control. She is absolutely terrified, and understandably so. If Julia goes to the police, I'll do the same. I'll explain exactly what's happened. I'll tell them that you've attacked me; I'll tell them about the insurance claim and why you're behaving the way you are. If it comes to that and you force me into that situation, then you won't see a penny from my book. You and I had an agreement . . . if you choose to break that agreement, then don't expect me to honour my side of it."

He looked quite flabbergasted by this eloquent and well rehearsed speech. He took a cigarette out and lighted it. His face contorted as he took a deep drag, inhaled, and deliberately blew the smoke into my face. Placing the cigarette back between his lips, he took a step forward towards me and stared at me with incomprehension. My mouth now had dried, I tried to swallow but couldn't, my whole body was quivering with fear waiting for what was undoubtedly going to be a violent onslaught. I almost wanted it to happen; to get it over with.

"Quite finished have you?" he said.
I didn't reply. I knew this was the prelude to something I wasn't going to enjoy.

"When do you expect to hear about the book . . . how much they're going to pay for it?"

"I don't know," I replied. "I've explained all to this you before. It could be a few days, a couple of weeks, I really don't know.

"Right," he said, deliberately blowing another lungful of smoke into my face, "I'll give you until the end of the month, unless you hear before of course. Let's hope the fucking thing sells . . . if it doesn't . . ."

"What do you mean by that?"

"You know exactly what I mean. You can tell the beautiful young Julia that you've got a reprieve until the end of the month . . . that should put her mind at rest."

"And you promise to keep away from Julia?"

"You have my word as an officer and a gentleman. Let us hope for both your sakes that they fall in love with your writing. If they don't then you know very well what's going to happen. I've told you . . . I don't intend to wait while you write another one. Now unless there's some other matter you wish to discuss . . ."

"No, I've said what I had to say . . . that's it," I said, the dryness of my mouth making it difficult to enunciate the words. I took a couple of cautious steps towards the door still expecting him to spring upon me. He turned towards the door, put his hand on the Yale lock and released the latch. His face was now a few inches away from mine, which allowed me a further close scrutiny of the angry pulsating veins in his forehead. The door opened and I retreated to the comparative safety of my room.

A minute or so later I heard him leaving: his door slamming, and his heavy plodding footsteps as he descending the stairs.

Well, I'd achieved my objective, I told myself. I'd stood up to this dangerous bully; told him whose boss . . . well almost. At least now I'd made my position clear to him in no uncertain terms. I ferreted around the room and found a half full bottle of water of indeterminate age under the bed. I took the cap off and swallowed the lot. The lingering taste of polythene and plastic was inconsequential; I was dehydrated to an extreme level; not just from fear, but a legacy from the celebration last night.

Now at least I could tell Julia with all honesty that I'd spoken to him. Not just spoken to him, I'd warned him to stay away, well until the end of the month anyway. I couldn't tell Julia that. I just had to hope that some good news would be forthcoming by then; I could then relay this to him and soon after that I'd give him whatever money I was offered and that would be the end of it.

If only it was this straightforward. Even looking on the positive side, if all of this went to plan, Julia would certainly want to see the acceptance letter. If we were together, which by the way things were headed, we probably would be: how could I explain the sudden disappearance of what could be a large sum of money? Sooner or later I'd have to come clean and tell her what I'd agreed to do. This was definitely a major stumbling block. The relationship between us had been re-ignited far too quickly. In a couple of month's time the whole deal could've been conducted without her ever knowing a thing about it. Why is life so bloody complicated?

After a few hours of futile procrastination I decided; I'd tell her the truth. The self imposed stress of all this subterfuge was making me into a nervous wreck. Yes . . . that's it . . . this evening . . . I'd tell her what was going on before things got even more complicated. The web that had been weaved was already tangled enough without making it worse. It was after all my money . . . assuming there would be some of course. If I wanted to give it to Stubbs, that was my choice; it was vitally important though for her to understand that I was doing so because I *wanted* to do so, not because of any threats from him. If she couldn't understand my motives then it would be pointless us being together.

Having finally arrived at this decision, I sat by my typewriter and started making notes for the sequel. This would include me and Stubbs and the whole ghastly business. There wouldn't be any difficulty in making the characters sound real: this would be written effortlessly from the heart.

A couple of hours later, having made copious notes, I started writing: Chapter one. . .

'Tim Williams wasn't imagining it, he was being followed' . . . yes that would be an intriguing way to start it, I convinced himself, and carried on. By lunchtime the first thousand words were written. I read through it several times and grinned with self satisfaction. Yes, it sounded real; it certainly wasn't difficult to put myself in the place of the protagonist. I continued for a further thirty minutes and then decided to celebrate this outstanding literary production with a pint over the road. I might even be tempted with a hot steaming plate of Shepherds pie if it was on offer. Everything now seemed to be fitting into place. Writing from first hand experience made things so much easier; perhaps Stubbs ought to be thanked for providing the material.

After carrying out a close examination of some disgusting looking macaroni cheese bubbling and fermenting under some low wattage light bulbs in a glass cabinet on the bar; my appetite rapidly evaporated. I settled for a couple of ham rolls and carried these and a pint of 'best' over to my usual table. For some reason things were going downhill fast at The Crown and Anchor; the attractive barmaid had been replaced (hopefully only temporarily) by a frumpy middle aged woman with a harelip and a large ugly mole on her cheek. Not only this; how could they expect to keep their loyal clientele when they'd substituted their delicious Shepherds pie for this revolting macaroni cheese dish which was the nearest thing to a dry rot sporophore that I'd ever seen.

I surreptitiously glimpsed around the bar to satisfy myself that Stubbs wasn't lurking somewhere; uncrumpled the first few pages of my new book and started reading through it again. Before I'd got to the end of the second page my peace was interrupted.

"Hello Tom," a voice could be heard saying.

I looked up and standing over the table was Eric . . . Eric Bottomly.

"I hope I'm not disturbing you, I just saw you sitting there by yourself and thought I'd just pop over and say hello as it were."

"Yes, of course," I said. Quite dumfounded as to why he should bother.

"How are you anyway . . . how's the book coming along?"

"Very well thanks, I'm just revising some stuff at the moment."

"Ooh I didn't mean to disturb you . . . I'll be on my way," he said.

"No, your not disturbing me, have a seat if you like," I said, convinced now beyond any doubt that Eric had evolved from a species of sea turtle.

"Yes . . . thank you I will then. I've always fancied myself doing what you're doing you know . . . becoming a writer. They say everyone's got a book in them."

"Yes they do, and that's probably where it should remain," I said.

After a few more disparaging comments, Eric now understood that I wasn't about to offer any enthusiasm or encouragement for any career change he might be contemplating. He got up nodded and bowed obsequiously, then floated out of the door.

Feeling slightly guilty at my callous condemnation of Eric's literary aspirations; I knocked back the remainder of my pint and left. Why was it? I asked myself, whenever anyone hears that you're writing, the first thing they say is 'ah yes I've always wanted to do that'. Everyone seems to imagine they have a natural talent and could do it. They were all born writers . . . they'd just chosen not to. They were all the new James Joyce, Kafka, or Dostoevsky; it's just they hadn't actually put pen to paper yet because of various time constraints etc, but one day . . .when they've got the time they'd write their memoirs. They'd had such interesting lives; people would be falling over themselves to buy their book . . . bastards! I muttered; my lip involuntarily curling with venom.

It was now just after two thirty. Back in my room in front of the typewriter, I felt an overwhelming urge to crawl into bed and recover a few hours lost sleep before seeing Julia. The problem with this would be waking up muzzy headed and full of self loathing knowing the afternoon should have been used more constructively. With a little effort I could write another thousand words . . .well if not a thousand, at least five hundred; a couple of pages. Think how much better I'll feel at six o'clock if I continue, I said to myself and started bashing the typewriter keys again.

At five thirty I pulled the last page I'd written from the typewriter sat back and went through the afternoons work. Yes, it read well, it was tense . . . a page turner . . . I'd definitely found the right formula. In my estimation

I'd written at least two thousand words. I had every right to go out and enjoy myself this evening. At this rate it would only take three months to write a sequel. I started reflecting upon the conversation I'd had with Eric in the pub earlier. What an arrogant pompous swine I must have sounded, I thought to myself. Poor pathetic creature had all his hopes dashed in a couple of sentences. How would I have felt being the recipient of such a scathing and dismissive denunciation? The problem with writing is, I reasoned, the solitude: the detachment, the lack of normal empathetic interaction with other people. Perhaps that explains why so many writers suffer mental problems, become chain smokers or alcoholics. Not many people could cope without becoming affected by it in some way or another. And then there's the rejection of course. People spend many months, often years, living an isolated and penurious existence struggling to produce something only to receive a pre-printed rejection slip. Yes . . . there's no doubt about it you have to be mad to do it. If you're not, you certainly will be after a few years. After this dismal summation, I placed the cover over my typewriter, stood by the door listening with my stethoscope for a few minutes, and then proceeded to carry out some serious ablutionary activity in preparation for my evening with Julia.

The twenty minute walk to Julia's flat should have offered a pleasant relaxing opportunity to unwind and get some fresh air, but half way there the heavy grey clouds opened up and released a torrential cloudburst. Had it had happened a couple of minutes earlier there would have been places to shelter from it, but now I just had to accept that I was going to get soaked and would arrive at her flat like a drowned rat. Had I not stopped and queued in the off-licence for wine and cigarettes, I would have just escaped it. 'Bloody country', I muttered to myself as my feet squelched in the saturated leather moccasins I was wearing.

"Good God, why didn't you get a taxi?" she said.

"Because it wasn't raining when I left."

"Didn't you hear the forecast? . . . They predicted this on the radio this morning."

"Oh it's just bloody typical; it's another of life's perverse conspiracies: If I'd have thought 'Oh I think it might rain, I'll jump in a taxi; it would've stayed fine. You just can't win. The sooner you realize this and stop trying to fight it, the easier it becomes to accept the measured amount of shit that is meted out to you regardless. It reminds me of the first line of the alcoholic's serenity prayer."

"Gosh you're getting very bitter in your old age," she said, giving me a friendly thump. "What's the first line of the prayer you're talking about anyway?"

"Oh it doesn't matter; something about accepting the things you cannot change. While we're on the subject of alcoholics, shall I open this?" I said, holding a bottle of Saint Emilion up.

"No, I've just opened one in the kitchen it's probably not anything like that, but we can save that for dinner; take your soaking wet jacket and shoes off and we'll go and have a chat in there. Did you speak to that horrible creepy man by the way?"

"Stubbs . . . you mean. Yes I did."

"What happened, what did you say?"

"Well nothing happened . . . I just told him that he'd been seen hanging around outside here . . . not just you . . . I said that your neighbour's had seen him as well, that you were frightened and about to go to the police and report him. I said . . ."

"What did he say?"

"Hang on; I'm just trying to tell you," I said, unable to disguise my annoyance at her predictable interruptions.

"I said that if it happens again, we'd both go straight to the police, and that was about it really."

"Didn't you ask him *why* he was lurking around outside here? Surely that would have been the thing to ask him: why didn't you ask him what he was doing?"

"Yes, I suppose you're right," I agreed. "The reason I didn't is that it would have been pretty pointless. I don't suppose he knows himself, and even if he did, he's hardly likely to tell me."

"Oh you are a Silly Billy," she said poking me in the chest, "that's the first thing you should've asked him . . . you could have gauged his reaction . . . heard what possible excuse he could've come up with. Do you see what I mean?"

I was becoming increasingly frustrated and annoyed. I'd done what she'd asked me to do; I'd exposed myself to all sorts of danger by speaking to him, I'd warned him to keep away from her, and now she was criticising the way I'd gone about it. I'd planned to tell her everything . . . and now . . . What was it with her? Why couldn't she just listen for a few moments instead of continually interrupting and making me feel incompetent? Well that was it, she'd had her chance to know the full story but now she'd blown it. I swallowed half a glass of red wine, lighted a cigarette, and sat ruefully examining the bright red toes poking through the holes in my socks as Julia starting cooking her version of Nasi Goreng . . . my favourite dish.

Chapter 6

The rain was still pouring from the heavens when I'd left Julia's flat at eight thirty the next morning. My light leather moccasins had taken on a weird shape where Julia in all her wisdom had placed them on the radiator overnight to dry. I felt strangely ambivalent about the whole thing. I'd been looking forward to seeing her and was mildly disappointed that I'd not been able to tell her the truth: to come clean with her and get things off my chest: but now I felt a blissful feeling of relief in getting away from her and getting back to my own sanctuary. Today, I decided, I'd phone my agent just to make sure they'd received my manuscript. With any luck I might glean some positive information. That would certainly give some added incentive to spend another lonely day in front of my typewriter.

By the time I'd arrived at Albion Mansions I was completely soaked to the skin again. 'Don't need to worry about phoning the agent' I said to myself, 'I'll probably die of pneumonia before the bloody book gets published anyway'.

After searching around through piles of papers, I eventually found the letter I was looking for with the agent's telephone number on it, I grabbed a pocket full of change which was piled up on the mantelpiece and went downstairs to make the call. Although it wasn't exactly private; the public payphone in the hall at Albion Mansions was useful. I just had to be a bit careful to make sure no one was hovering around nearby who might listen in to my conversation . . . particularly Stubbs.

After having exhausted the supply of coins I'd placed on top of the payphone waiting to speak to Jane Phillips my agent; I finally heard 'sorry to have kept you, just putting you through' a second or two before I was about to petulantly bang the receiver down and give up.

"Hello Tom," she said, "Nice to hear from you, I'm pleased you called; yes I have received your manuscript and I've now read through it. I'm quite optimistic that we can do something with this; I've already spoken to a publisher that has expressed some interest, so let's keep our fingers crossed."

"Oh that's excellent news," I replied glancing around furtively to make sure I wasn't being overheard.

"I'm having lunch with him tomorrow and I'll let you know how it goes. If you want to give me a call after the weekend I might have some more news on it for you."

"Yes of course," I replied, trying to suppress my elation. . . . "And thanks for everything."

It occurred to me that there were still nearly two weeks until the end of the month. It was just possible that I might have an offer for the book by then. Was it possible that I might actually see a cheque from them by then? I really had no idea how these things worked. The small sums I'd been paid for the articles and short stories I'd written before seem to take ages to come through. Perhaps this would be different. The more I thought about it, the more I realized it wasn't exactly a matter of such urgency. If I were to show Stubbs the letter confirming the offer, that should be good enough. Stubbs would have to wait like everyone else. Oh of course . . . there was another problem; I remembered: I still hadn't told Julia the truth. Reflecting upon the conversation we'd had last night, I had to admit she was right. I should have asked Stubbs why he was hanging around her flat. She was absolutely correct. She'd hit a raw nerve. Had she of known exactly how volatile and dangerous Stubbs could be, she wouldn't have asked me this, she would have understood. I was just making the situation more difficult for myself. It was ridiculous that I should be irritated by such a normal path of reasoning. Today was Thursday: I'd be seeing her again tomorrow night; I'd tell her the whole story then. No more excuses.

Fired with a renewed burst of enthusiasm, I returned to my room and continued writing. For the first hour or so the words flowed effortlessly. The writing though, gradually slowed up as my brain was being incessantly bombarded with a plethora of conflicting thoughts and ominous messages. I got up and stretched, looked out of the window and then lighted a cigarette, pacing up and down the room like a deranged predator; I tried to find some order to my thinking; to get things into perspective. The biggest worry; the thing troubling me most, would be the terrible anticlimax if after all of this, the book was turned down. This, if I could pin point it, was what was causing me so much consternation. If this happened I could cope . . . but what would the consequences be as far as Stubbs was concerned? I daren't think about it. The second major problem was trying to get Julia to understand why I wanted to give Stubbs the money. My moral and ethical reasoning was all very well, but there were limits. Yes, I had already fully anticipated precisely how she would react and this would not only ruin the weekend we'd planned together, but would probably destroy any faith she had in my judgement in the future. She might also conclude that I'd offered Stubbs the money because I was scared of him . . . scared of what he might do. This would be totally unacceptable.

On the positive side: if she understood my reasoning; my guilt for having placed Stubbs in this invidious predicament, she would not only understand, she might even respect my compassion. Of course she'd need time to assimilate the facts of the case; wouldn't anyone? Yes things probably weren't quite as black as they seemed. Once she'd had time to consider it, she'd be able to live with it. Once the money had been paid over, I could carry on writing with a free mind . . . complete the sequel, and everyone would be happy. Thank God, I said, trying to convince myself; at least there is a positive scenario to all of this.

Suddenly the room seemed to take on a stifling claustrophobic air. I could hear Stubbs moving around next door. The air was thin, it was becoming difficult to breathe; I had to get out . . .out into the fresh air, see the sky . . .space . . .space to move freely, to walk, to run, to be near people . . .strangers . . .it didn't matter.

Although I knew Stubbs was next door, I couldn't wait to listen with my stethoscope before opening my door; I just had to get out . . . and fast.

Within sixty seconds I was standing on the pavement outside. I looked around briefly and then started to walk. After a minute or so the walk broke into a run. Soon I was down on the sea front. I stood for a few moments clutching the iron balustrade separating the promenade from the beach. The light persistent rain beat unrelentingly against my face as I inhaled as much as my lungs would take in of the briny air. The fierce dirty grey sea, the seagulls squawking excitedly overhead and the heavy black clouds above assuaged my troubled mind. After a few minutes, I could breathe again. My eyes were stinging from the rain, my head pounding like a steam engine. I started walking again into the wind. The chill of it didn't matter, I felt free and alive once more.

In the distance I could see a group of people sheltering under the canopy of a sea front cafe. As it grew closer, the aroma of coffee and fried onions filled my nostrils with delight. The temptation was too much. The thought of a polystyrene cup of steaming coffee and a slimy hot dog was irresistible. Devouring this like a starving animal and wiping the residue of the French mustard and tomato ketchup from my hands, I now felt rejuvenated. Life wasn't so bad after all.

Nothing like a good healthy walk, I told myself as I climbed the ten flights of stairs back up to my room. The throbbing and pounding inside my head had eased and the general feeling of claustrophobia inside the room had abated. After a couple of cigarettes I sat back in front of my typewriter and continued.

The whole afternoon was spent dedicated to the cause. By seven o'clock another two thousand words had been added to my new book. It was definitely coming along in leaps and bounds. Hopefully Stubbs didn't read this sort of book I thought; describing him, or a facsimile of him, as a demented psychopath wouldn't contribute much to the already strained situation between us. The gong announcing dinner must have sounded at least ten minutes ago. A quick check with the stethoscope confirmed it was safe to leave and I made my way downstairs.

Eric Bottomly, Benson and the other half boarders were all ensconced at their usual tables as I entered the dining room. I gave them all a quick nod in the style of a famous celebrity and settled myself at my table. I would have preferred to have seen Stubbs as well sitting by his table in the corner. The fact that he wasn't there yet meant that he'd have to pass my table to get to his; which necessitated trying to avoid any possible eye contact with him. Normally it wasn't a problem as I'd learned to arm myself with a newspaper to hold up, but today I hadn't bought one. Another trick I'd mastered was to dive under the table when I saw Stubbs entering the dining room, as if trying to retrieve something that had dropped from the table. Although effective, this diversionary tactic was best saved for emergencies.

Mrs Hoskins was in good spirits; no doubt the obvious appreciation of her home made Irish stew was a contributory factor in her buoyant demeanour this evening. I was so engrossed in savouring the delights of this that I hardly noticed Stubbs brush past me to take up his position. Judging from the satisfied expressions on the faces of the half boarders one might imagine that they would have been happy had this been the only dish she ever cooked. The home made apple pie and custard was always a close runner up of course. Even the morose looking Jack always devoured two helpings of it as he sat at a table just a couple of feet from the kitchen with rows of pliers and pincers dangling from his belt.

Having scooped up the last it, I studied the reflection of Stubbs in the glass door of the welsh dresser in front of me. He was still wading through his bowl of stew, which meant it would be safe to leave and make my way back to my room. I got up slowly, walked over to the kitchen and thanked Mrs Hoskins; complimented her once again on her culinary expertise, and left.

Sometimes the evenings were a problem. After a full days writing, I felt tired; too tired to read, yet not tired enough to want to sleep. There was no television in my room and neither did I want one. I did have a small radio, and some evenings I would listen to a play, or perhaps a current affairs programme. It was still early, not yet eight o'clock, and at times like this I missed Julia. We used to sit for hours together talking about something or other and the evening would fly by. Perversely though, after a few evenings with her, I relished the prospect of solitude once more. Perhaps there never would be a happy medium. You see it in films; read about it in books, but in real life . . .?"

I'd always believed that men and women were incompatible. The only way it could ever satisfactorily work in the long term would be if both partners were congenitally simple. Yes that was absolutely vital. If both partners were incredibly easy going with extremely limited aspirations, then it might stand half a chance. Boring, unadventurous, parochial yes these were the sort of 'qualities' required to co-exist. Eternally grateful to have a little house; one they've bought together, a 'comfortable' home that in twenty five years would be theirs. The most important prerequisite of all was of course, a good job. Not just a good job, but a good pension to go with it. The prospect of striving to achieve this; to have smug fatuous friends visit every so often sitting around on your new 'leather look' three piece suite uttering facile platitudes whilst gawking at your holiday snaps, after two weeks in Benidorm or some other disgusting place. Oh yes, *Abigail's party* personified. There *must* be more to life than this I muttered.

'Oh well', I said out loud, 'life itself is a compromise'. The prospect of ending up in thirty years time eking out a lonely existence in the top floor of Albion Mansions was even less appealing. I'd had one very close shave last year with Julia: nearly fallen into the trap of been slowly sucked in by the pernicious all embracing quick sands of normality and conformity and escaped. I knew it was going to happen again, so why bother to fight it? I knew I could cope with it, I might even enjoy the 'togetherness' whatever that meant, provided I could do what I wanted to do . . . to write; to be totally free from these iniquitous greedy grasping financial institutions. If the writing didn't work, the prospect of having to go back and work for the insurance company for another thirty years was unthinkable. I'd given them over fifteen years of my life and bitterly resented every day of it.

A long held dream of mine was to enjoy the pleasures of both worlds. The idea of being a best selling author, living in an old rambling country house with an oak panelled study full of books would be perfect. A few literary lunches, book signings, and the occasional appearance on some media programme . . .

yes that wouldn't be *too* unpleasant. Even the notion of having children around could even be tolerated, provided of course they were impeccably behaved, had suitably polished faces and kept out of the way most of the time.

But back to reality; it was now nine fifteen; I read through the days work again and was reasonably happy with it. A few alterations perhaps might provide greater impact, but not now . . . it could wait until tomorrow. In a semi inebriated state last Wednesday, I'd suggested that we should go away for the weekend together. Of course Julia jumped at the idea. At the time it seemed quite appealing; to get away from the old boring familiar surroundings for a couple of days, but now I was beginning to panic: I hadn't arranged anything. There was a country hotel in the new forest that had been advertising special weekend breaks for a modest amount; I'd torn the advert out of the newspaper and put it somewhere 'just in case'. All I had to do now was to remember where the hell I'd put it.

An hour later, after having turned the whole room upside down; I found it in the last place I looked . . . underneath my typewriter. Immediately after breakfast tomorrow I'd phone them and make the booking. Julia was going to finish at lunch time: I'd agreed to get round to her flat by two o'clock which meant I might be able to devote a few hours to the book before we left.

Now suitably exhausted from the days activities, I settled down for the night. For once, in a very long time I managed to fall asleep immediately and slept soundly until five thirty the next morning. It wasn't the vibrating pane of glass that woke me; it was the commotion coming from next door. I sat up and listened, I couldn't quite make it out . . . a sort of chanting and wailing sound. I jumped out of bed, walked over to the door, and placed my stethoscope against the dividing wall between myself and Stubbs. Nothing could be heard. I stood in position for another few minutes but all was quiet. I must have been dreaming I thought; climbed back into bed and tried to get back to sleep. I'd just drifted off when it started again. This time I could hear Stubbs clearly shouting in his menacing voice, 'Just wait, alright then, just you bloody wait . . . you think I don't know what's happening, just you wait.' After listening for another ten minutes it seemed to go quiet again. I carefully opened my door and placed the stethoscope against a panel in his door. I could hear snoring sounds interspersed by what sounded like apnoea. I realized that he'd been having a nightmare. A cold chill ran down my spine when I began contemplating the seriously disturbed frame of mind that had prompted this eerie psychotic tirade.

I tried to put this out of my mind. Concentrate on the day that had just begun. It was now a quarter to seven. I crept out to the bathroom, washed, shaved and crept back to my room. In half an hour I'd go out and buy a newspaper, this would take my mind of things for a bit . . . then it would be time for breakfast. Mustn't think about Stubbs, I said to myself: soon . . . very soon, the whole wretched business will be over.

Booking the hotel was easy enough. The only thing I objected to was having to book in as Mr and Mrs Dunford. I didn't want Julia jumping to conclusions.

Being thoroughly disorganised and in fairness preoccupied with other matters, I'd forgotten to make the once weekly pilgrimage to the launderette. After conducting an in depth search of various cupboards and drawers it quickly became apparent I'd run out of clean clothes. Some sort of contingency measures were required. The prospect now of sitting in the foul smelling launderette for a couple of hours was abhorrent. The alternative wasn't particularly appealing either; it meant a dreaded shopping trip. Unpleasant though it was; this was definitely the least of two evils. At least if carried out with military precision, this would be quick, in forty five minutes I could be back in front of my typewriter and could write a few more pages before leaving.

Initially, when I set out the weather was reasonable; dark grey overcast skies with a slight westerly wind. A typical January day. Within the blink of an eye something changed: the wind became fierce and gusty, it grew much darker; a sudden crack of thunder, then gigantic lumps of ice dropped from the heavens, hitting cars like a shower of bullets. Umbrellas appeared from nowhere opening up like massive flower petals as the ice bounced off the pavements. At first I tried to ignore it: pretend it wasn't happening, but soon I had to stop and take shelter. The hailstones pelting down were stinging my face with lumps of ice running down the back of my neck. I was under attack; somebody up there'd got it in for me, what more proof you need than this? What perfect weather to choose for a romantic weekend in the country!

Five minutes later, the shower eased off sufficiently to allow me to continue. I had though, sustained a couple of minor injuries in the scuffle to find shelter. The first was to my right eye where a woman erecting an umbrella had in her panic, allowed one the spikes to nearly poke my eye out. The second was to my leg where another woman with a double buggy containing two red faced babies had scraped my ankle. Once inside the relative safety of Marks and Spencer I ran around like a man possessed; desperate to buy the things I needed and get out.

Half an hour later I was back in front of the typewriter with a constant trickle of water running off me onto the threadbare carpet surrounding my desk. It had to be said that I had now become conditioned into accepting each misfortune bestowed upon me with an almost dignified and resigned stoicism.

By lunch time I'd managed a further three and a half pages. I stuffed the new clothes into an old travel holdall, locked my door and headed off to Julia's flat. It had crossed my mind to get a taxi but as I was already soaked, it hardly mattered now.

Julia's initial castigatory reprimand for my sodden appearance was followed by a hug that left me breathless.

"Why didn't you take an umbrella with you this morning?"

"Because it wasn't raining when I left."

"But that's why you take them, in case it rains" she said as if addressing a child and obviously exasperated by my foolishness.

"Well, that might be true, but I didn't, and anyway they're dangerous. There ought to be a test; then a licence issued before you can use them. Look . . . here look at this . . ." I showed her my eye which was still slightly red and smarting.

"Oh I don't know, you are the absolute limit. Other people seem to manage to carry out simple things, but for you, everything's a problem. Did you remember to book the hotel?"

"Yes, it's all arranged. They did explain that they've had a few problems down there but they were now getting themselves together again."

"What do they mean by 'problems'."

"Oh nothing really, just a touch of salmonella and legionnaires disease I think they said."

Julia had become accustomed to my flippancy and simply ignored this. It didn't take long though for the light hearted bickering to start which was an inherent constituent of our relationship. We were nonetheless both delighted to be together as we headed west at a snails pace in her battered old Fiesta. It rained ceaselessly throughout the journey; only one wiper bade was working properly on the passenger side. Finally, after two and a half hours we arrived at The New Forest Inn.

"We have a reservation," I stated to the anorexic looking girl at the reception area.

"Ah yes sir, what name is it?"

"Dunford; Mr and Mrs Dunford," I replied trying to keep a straight face as Julia was poking me in the ribs. Julia's husky laugh had obviously given the game away as we carted our bags up to the first floor. I looked behind me and immediately detected the bemused expression on the face of the young girl.

"I think you've given the game away," I said, "She definitely knows we're not married."

"What makes you think that?"

"It's just the way she was looking at us."

"Who cares? Perhaps she's just envious. Not many girls have the chance to spend an illicit weekend in the country with a famous writer."

The room we'd been given was a surprise. A magnificent king sized four poster bed dominated the space with an immaculate white bathroom en suite. Sachets of scents and bath oils were strategically positioned throughout. Large white fluffy towels were piled up invitingly on a stool. Hanging on the door, were a couple of thick white dressing gowns with the hotel logo stitched onto on the pockets.   A pair of French doors opened up onto a small balcony overlooking acres of green fields. I was beginning to wonder if the receptionist had made a mistake. I couldn't relax until I knew. On the pretext of making sure that the car was locked, I went downstairs and checked with the receptionist.

"I just wanted to confirm," I said nervously, "I booked a room for two nights assuming it was part of the 'special deal' you advertised. Are you sure we are in the right room?"

"Why? Is there something wrong? The receptionist asked looking worried.

"No it's fine," I replied somewhat embarrassed by my limited means. "What time does the restaurant open?"

"At seven thirty sir."

"Thanks," I said, and retreated back to the room.

Julia was already stretched out in the four poster and suggested we should put it to the test before dinner.

At eight o'clock we reluctantly extricated ourselves from the sumptuous bed, enjoyed the benefits of a really deep bubble bath and went down to the restaurant. The dim lighting and soft classical music that greeted us created a pretentiously genteel and comforting ambience. Although there were only two other couples in there, we were shown to our table by a humourless bald headed waiter who I suggested was probably an acid bath murderer. This started Julia off with a fit of the giggles which she was unable to suppress. Once the snorting and guffawing had subsided a little, the waiter returned and presented us each with a large leather bound menu, and a separate leather bound wine list for me.

As soon as I opened the menu, I realized that my initial suspicions were justified. The set price for dinner for the two of us exceeded the cost of the room for the two nights and this was without wine. We couldn't very well get up and leave now . . . we were trapped: sitting ducks . . . lambs to the slaughter. It really wouldn't have been appropriate now for me to announce my shock at seeing these prices, I just muttered 'bastards' under my breath, which Julia had become accustomed to and accepted it, as one might a nervous tic.

After a few minutes the waiter returned and took our order. The next question was 'had sir had a chance to 'peruse' the wine list'? I had indeed, but this was adding insult to injury. Why should I be expected to pay three times the off licence price for a bottle of Saint Emilion? Apart from that, one bottle wouldn't go anywhere. After all we were supposed to be relaxing and enjoying ourselves.

"Do you have a house wine?" I enquired.

"A house wine sir?" the waiter repeated, lifting his nose in the air as if trying to avoid some foul smell coming up from the table.

"Would sir like a whole bottle or just a half perhaps?"

"Sir would like two bottles of it, 'red ones,' I replied.

"Stop it," Julia said, "I know he's obnoxious, but behave yourself for once or we'll get thrown out. We don't have to eat in here tomorrow night anyway. We'll go into the town and find an Indian."

"What do we need an Indian for?" I enquired. "I thought we were quite happy by ourselves."

"Stop it," Julia said, worried now that I was about to have an altercation with the waiter when he returned.

Within a short space of time the two bottles of house wine were placed on the table. With extreme care the cork was removed from the first one and a little was poured for me to taste. The waiter then obsequiously enquired as to whether he should open the second bottle to allow it to breathe, or if I would prefer to wait.

"No, you can open it," I replied. "It won't get a chance to catch it's breath with us around."

"Of course sir," the waiter replied disdainfully; purposely choosing to ignore my attempted witticism.

The food arrived fairly quickly after this. The prawn cocktail starter clearly wasn't a speciality of this restaurant. I found three prawns the size of tadpoles buried in a revolting mixture of salad cream and tomato sauce. The Chateaubriand main course was slightly better, it did at least taste of meat, and there was enough of it.

Half way through the second bottle of wine, I decided to tell Julia the truth about Stubbs. I'd wanted to put it off again so that we could get away from the whole wretched business, but I knew it had to come out. The more I kept putting it off the worse it would become.

"There's something I was going to tell you," I began.

"Something you *were* going to tell me. Does that mean you've decided not to then?"

"No, don't be pedantic. I mean something I am going to tell you."

"Sorry, go on then, I can't wait to hear it, whatever it is."

"Well it's about that fellow Vince . . . actually I call him Stubbs, but that doesn't really matter. When I was with the insurance company five years ago, I was in charge of the claims department as you know. Well one of the claims I handled was from him. It was for a big fire . . . buildings and contents insurance . . . and . . ."

"Oh come on, get to the point," she interrupted.

"Yes, well his house was completely destroyed. Although he was technically insured, there were certain inaccuracies on the proposal form . . . the declaration . . . which meant we had a good reason not to pay out on his claim."

"Okay, I understand. What happened, how much was his claim for then?"

"Just under half a million."

Julia went quiet. The relaxed happy expression on her face altered dramatically. She, having a woman's intuition, had already got the picture. "Oh Christ," she said, "this is why he was following you isn't it. "Oh God, this is why he's been hanging around outside my flat . . . What the hell's he doing living in your building? Oh Christ I don't like the sound of this, it's like some horror film."

"There's a bit more to it, let me finish. Evidently his wife died in the fire trying to rescue their daughter. He showed me the photographs of the charred remains of the property and of his wife and daughter. Of course I'm dreadfully sorry that he lost his wife, and that his daughter . . . she got quite badly burned, and again, I saw the photos of her, it was really horrific . . . but . . ."

"Oh for God's sake Tom do get to the point. This is awful. Why didn't you settle his claim? What is it he wants from you now?"

"Well he doesn't blame me for the fire obviously, or for the fact that he lost his wife, or that his daughter was injured; what he blames me for is finding a loophole if you like, for not paying out on the claim. He lost everything . . . every penny he'd ever worked for was in the house. He didn't have a mortgage on it, it was paid for. Evidently he was a successful photographer; the room he used as a studio was razed to the ground. All his cameras and photographic equipment were totally destroyed. He's been through a terrible experience; apparently he had a complete nervous breakdown . . . it is an awful story."

"Oh God," she said almost on the verge of tears. "I can't believe this. What was the reason you used for refusing to pay him?"

"I feel terrible about it now . . . it was my job . . . there was nothing personal to it. I had to go through

131

each claim over a certain amount and see if everything was as stated on the proposal form . . . you know . . . all the details . . . previous claims history that sort of thing, and I discovered that a previous claim he'd made was *just* within the last five years. Only a few days within the period; but nonetheless that was enough for the company to refuse to pay out."

"Oh God that's absolutely wicked, it's totally immoral. Why didn't you just let the claim go through; nobody would have bothered to check would they?"

"They could have done; and bearing in mind it was such a large sum of money, they probably would have. I'm sorry now that I didn't just authorize the payment, but that's by the way now."

"Oh you are a fool, why didn't you tell me all of this before? I really don't understand you sometimes. What's he planning to do . . . revenge . . . is that what it's all about? That's what he's looking for isn't it?"

"Well that's true it was, I suppose, but when he told me the story I felt completely devastated, racked with guilt. If I could somehow turn the clock back of course, I would let the claim go through . . . but . . ."

"I don't understand, you're saying it *was* revenge; what do you mean?"

"Well, after I'd had time to think about it, I decided I wanted to do something to help him. You may think I'm crazy but I've offered to give him any money I get for the book if it's successful. He was saying that I've ruined his life, and in many ways that's true. The money from the insurance wouldn't have brought his wife back, or stopped his daughter's pain and suffering, but as he says quite rightly; he could have tried to rebuild his life to some extent."

Julia stared at me for a few moments still in shock over these revelations. The bald headed waiter hovered a few feet away from our table clearly desperate to hear the rest of the story. Mildly embarrassed knowing that we knew he'd been listening, he sauntered over to the table and poured the remainder of the wine into our glasses.

"Would sir like another bottle perhaps?"

"No thanks," I replied: "just the bill please."

"Yes, I can understand you feeling like that I suppose; but what if your book isn't successful?"

"Well then there's nothing I can do. I don't have any money to give him, that's the only thing I could suggest."

"I still don't understand though," she said looking frightened, "If he's not looking for some form of retribution; why is he still hanging around outside *my* flat. What have *I* got to do with it anyway? Oh God . . . I think we ought to go straight to the police. I think we ought to leave here now and go and tell the police exactly what's been going on. The man is obviously mentally ill. You *are* telling me everything now aren't you?"

"Yes of course. Look . . . there is one thing though I haven't mentioned. I phoned my agent yesterday and she's quite hopeful that the book will be sold. She was seeing a publisher today who's already expressed some interest in it and I've got to phone her again early next week."

"Oh that's terrific; I'm so pleased for you . . . really; but I still think . . ."

"No, I interrupted, I've spoken to Stubbs, or Vince as you call him and explained that things look quite promising. It's possible . . . just possible that I could have some sort of deal with the publisher by the end of this month. If this happens then I'll show the letter to him; he'll see that that I'm keeping to my word and that will put his mind at rest. I don't know how long it will take for any monies to come through, but at least it'll prove that I'm being honourable."

"Oh I don't know," she said, now looking more worried than ever.

"The whole point is that having made the offer, I want to honour it. If I, or we, were to go to the police now, he would automatically assume that it was because I'd changed my mind about giving him the money. That could make things a lot worse. That . . . believe me would be extremely unwise."

"Yes, I can see what you're saying. But really you should have gone to the police in the first place . . . you know . . . before you offered him the money; don't you think?"

"Maybe, but I felt so guilty by the way he was treated, it would have been like kicking him again while he's down. I just felt I wanted to do something to help."

I couldn't now explain the real truth; the fact that he'd violently attacked me, or the fact that the money from my book was offered in the desperate hope of saving my life. I couldn't possibly tell her what he'd said to me about losing someone you love. Or for that matter, that he'd had agreed to wait until the end of the month before doing God knows what to me and possibly to her. What a hole I'd dug for myself I thought while Julia was in the cloakroom.

"How much do you think they'll pay you for the book?" she asked on her return.

"I really have no idea."

"The thing that worries me most of all is what was in his mind when he was outside my flat. If he was happy to accept your apologies for the insurance thing; and if what you say is true, that he now accepts your offer of the monies from your book, then why . . .?"

"I don't know. I've told you though; I've told him that if he dares to go near your flat again that we will both go to the police. I also told him in no uncertain terms that if he forces us to do that, then he won't see a penny from me. He does understand that. I really think we ought to leave things as they are. Let me see what's happening with this publishing deal; I'll then talk to him again, and that I'm sure will be the end of it. If we went to the police now it would definitely exacerbate the situation. If he doesn't behave himself then I quite agree we'll do that. It'll then be him who's broken the agreement. I've made that abundantly clear to him already."

"I just hope you're right." she said, still looking frightened and unconvinced.

Chapter 7

Despite the black cloud hanging over us, we still managed to enjoy our short break away. The facilities at the hotel weren't exactly as advertised: the tennis court was overgrown with weeds and the net had virtually rotted away. The indoor swimming pool hadn't been completed, and the horse riding school didn't open until Easter. Not that it mattered much as the rain poured down constantly throughout our stay, any ideas we'd had of pleasant country walks had to be abandoned.

The worst part of it for me was paying the bill. Not only did it completely clean me out; but I had to ignominiously borrow twenty pounds from Julia. I firmly believed that the mysterious indefinable conspiracy working against us had triumphed again as the sun finally appeared five minutes before we were about to leave. 'It's up there laughing its bloody head off' I said, as I pointed accusingly up to the sky like a madman.

The drive back to Brighton was even slower than the journey down. Neither of us was particularly ecstatic about returning to the unknown. On the outskirts of Chichester we stopped at a country pub for a drink and something that was euphemistically referred to as a 'ploughman's', which I was still cursing about when we finally pulled up outside Julia's flat. The fact that she had to pay for that as well did little to lift my spirits. At least the sun was shining now; the weather was reasonably mild almost like a spring day. After unloading Julia's gigantic suitcase and my meagre holdall, we decided to go for a stroll along the seafront. The jubilant atmosphere between us had quelled noticeably. A certain tension was in the air. We were both undoubtedly thinking along the same lines but neither of us wanted to talk about it. I also realized that having agreed to hand over to Stubbs any money I might have made from the book, any hopes or dreams Julia might have been nurturing of our future together were now pretty dismal. In the end it was Julia who made the first move.

"Do you think you'll stay on at Albion Mansions?"

"I'm not sure; I've started writing another book, I'm determined to succeed at it. I couldn't honestly face going back into the insurance business . . . or for that matter any other form of commerce. The whole system's corrupt and I don't want any part of it. I'd rather starve than go back to that. "

"No, I understand, I was just wondering though . . .if you wanted you could move in with me; I'm at work all day . . .you'd still have your peace . . .you know . . .be able to write. I can see that's what you want to do; I'm not going to pressurize you into doing anything you don't want to do. It just seems a bit of a waste our being apart. There's no doubt you are an annoying cantankerous little sod, but we do get on . . . don't we?"

"Yes, yes we do. Perhaps I ought to sought this business out with Stubbs first. It is a bit delicate . . . I don't want him to think that I'm trying to run away if you see what I mean. Once that's done, then yes I think we have a better understanding than we did before and I don't see why this time it shouldn't work."

"Do you mean it?" she said.

"Of course."

"Oh that's great," she said stopping me in my tracks to give me a bone crushing hug.

"The only problem I can see is finding some space to work. If you remember it was difficult when I tried before . . . your flat is small . . . I mean there's no space to swing a cat. Perhaps I ought to buy a garden shed. Do you think anyone would mind if I did that?"

"Are you serious?"

"Of course, Somerset Maughan seemed to manage pretty well, and at least that way all my stuff wouldn't clutter up the flat."

"Well I can ask the letting agents if anyone would mind and see what they say if you like."

"Yes, it's worth a try."

I was both relieved and delighted at Julia's apparent acceptance that I was going to write and not ever go back to the insurance company. I hadn't forgotten exactly how difficult things had been between us before; the arguments and general bickering that had occurred over 'your papers being everywhere'. Naturally I was a little circumspect about reigniting the same problem. Other compromises would have to be made: if I wasn't going to be allowed to put a small shed in the garden, any writing I wanted to do would have to be whilst Julia was at work . . .literally nine until five; and definitely not at weekends. Julia; despite all her lovable qualities couldn't understand that creative writing required concentration. Her flat really was far too small for the two of us anyway. Perhaps if things went according to plan we could rent or even buy an old house with enough rooms to allow me the privacy I needed.

Slowly the day drew to a close. Although Julia tried to persuade me to move in with her immediately, she had to agree that it was sensible for me to sort this business out with Stubbs. The last thing she wanted was Stubbs hanging around her flat wanting to speak to me. No, once it had been settled and I'd paid him the monies as agreed, we'd be completely free of him. We could enjoy our new life together. I'd also paid Mrs Hoskins up until the end of the month so that would fit in nicely. The whole plan hinged upon receiving some positive news from my agent within the next few days.

Arriving back at Albion Mansions, I felt like a prisoner who'd been released on parole for a weekend. I'd just unpacked my bag when the dinner gong sounded. Oh shit, I thought, another tense encounter with Stubbs again. It was too quick; I hadn't had time to adjust. Had things had been different I would have spent the evening with Julia at her flat. The problem with this was her suggestion of getting a take away. Having run out of money, I couldn't let her pay for another meal; that would have been unbearable. Another potential difficulty with this would be that being as unpredictable as he was, Stubbs might suddenly appear outside her flat if I failed to appear to be in residence at Albion Mansions. No, I'd made the right decision; it was just a case of being patient for another few days.

After the short break away, sitting in the familiar surroundings of Mrs Hoskins dining room with all the other 'half boarders' in position, I was considering how easy it would be to become institutionalized here. The seedy yet reassuring aura of Albion Mansions was strangely comforting but also stifling at the same time.

Mrs Hoskins had somehow become a mother figure to all of us. The predictability, the regularity, the breakfast gong at eight o'clock, the dinner gong at seven o'clock . . . certain dishes on certain nights, always served at exactly the same time. Bath nights; everyone had their own bath time. There were undoubtedly many aspects of all of this I would miss. Had Stubbs not have appeared on the scene when he did, it would have been quite a wrench to detach myself from it. Living with Julia again of course had many advantages, but for me now, leaving Albion Mansions was not unlike a child having to go out and face the big dangerous world. Perhaps it was good that change was about to happen. Perhaps Stubbs had done me a favour.

Peace of mind and contentment were ever elusive states. I knew at the back of my mind that nothing really had changed as far as Julia's aspirations were concerned. She'd made the right noises, anything to placate me for the moment, a form of subtle capitulation; but it was all still there. Marriage, children, Sunday afternoon tea with the in-laws, Oh yes, I knew the way she thought! No doubt she was prepared to be patient a little longer, to tolerate my whims, my foolhardy misguided writing pretensions. Sooner or later I'd come back down to earth with a bang, learn to accept the cruel face of reality. Maybe my book *will* find a publisher, maybe I will write others, but trying to make a decent living at writing is something very few writers ever achieve. Best let me discover this for myself, was undoubtedly what she'd thought, I concluded.

Still, now there was no going back. The course of my life was indelibly mapped out. It had to work; there wouldn't be a third chance. The prospect of still being at Albion Mansions in twenty years time with a Mrs Hoskins floating around on a Zimmer was even more unpalatable.

After the soft luxurious king sized bed at hotel, I found it difficult to get to sleep in my hard cramped single bed. I was tossing and turning all night just wanting the morning to appear. Being unable to contain the suspense; immediately after breakfast I telephoned my agent. This time I got through to her straight away.

"Ah good news Tom," she said, "we've got a deal, I was going to suggest we meet up over lunch one day this week and I can explain what's on offer in more detail."

"Yes, yes," I said, unable to find my voice. "Can you tell me roughly what it is; I mean how much?"

"Yes of course," she replied, "the initial offer is for fifty thousand pounds, but that's based on a two book deal. It might be possible to squeeze a bit more, but that's what I wanted to talk to you about. What it means in simple terms is that you'd receive twenty five thousand immediately and another twenty five if you can write a sequel of similar quality. I said I thought this might be acceptable but that I'd obviously need to speak to you and then get back to them."

"Oh that's fantastic, there's no need for you to try for any more on my account; I'd be quite happy to accept that."

"Okay, I'll press on and get some contracts organized. I'm really pleased for you and let me wish you my heartfelt congratulations. Now which day would be good for you? I'm actually free on Wednesday, if you'd like to come up to our office at say twelve thirty, one o'clock we can meet up and have a chat about things over a bite to eat."

"Yes that's fine, and thanks for everything. Oh one last thing, I'm sorry to ask you this, but how soon can I have the money?"

"Well usually it takes a few weeks to get everything organised but I'll work as fast as I can for you. We can go through it all on Wednesday."

"Yes, yes, I'll look forward to it," I said, trying to stop my hand from shaking as I replaced the receiver.

This was it. This was the dream come true. I walked out into the street, I had to tell someone . . . Julia . . . yes, I had to tell her . . . right now. I couldn't phone from Albion Mansions and keep talking about such large sums of money, somebody might overhear. I walked to the end of the road and found a phone box. After directory enquiries had found the number for me I tried to dial it three times, my hand shaking to such an extent that I kept hitting the wrong numbers. Finally I heard Julia's husky voice.

"I've cracked it," I shouted manically.

"God Tom cracked what, what's happened?"

"The book, they want it and another one; fifty grand."

"You're joking," she said after a long pause.

"No honestly, it's true. I'm going up to London on Wednesday to tie it all up."

"Oh Tom that's wonderful, I can't believe it, that's fantastic. Hey, but wait; you're not going to give all that money to that creepy Vince are you?"

"No, no, of course not. Look; are you free at lunch time? We'll meet up."

"Yes, I'll have an early lunch. I'll see you outside here at twelve thirty if that's okay."

"Yes that's fine; I'll be waiting for you."

"Okay, I must go now . . . and Tom that's terrific news."

I didn't quite know what to do with myself. It was now only nine thirty, I wouldn't be seeing Julia for another three hours. I was far too excited to go back and sit in front of my typewriter. I found it hard to think clearly. This is it . . . this is everything I'd ever dreamt about. It really was happening. I stood for a few moments grinning outside the phone box trying to work out my next move. A walk . . . yes, a walk might help me to think . . . I thought, and headed down towards the sea front.

A dazzling bright sun appeared for brief moments from behind the fast moving clouds, a stiff breeze cutting through me did nothing to dampen my euphoria. Life was good again. I had everything now to look forward to. Everything to live for. There *was* a God after all. The sequel, ah yes the sequel . . . I'd already started it . . . written the first chapter. Suddenly a cold chill ran through me. What was Julia saying . . . you're not going to give all that money to Stubbs? That was it. No of course I wasn't. I'd agreed to give him the money from *'the book'*, the first book that was the deal. Twenty five grand after all is not exactly small sum of money by any account. Mind you there were certain costs to come out of this, the agent would want her fifteen per cent and then a certain amount had to be put aside for tax. That would take care of about eight thousand pounds, and then I needed some money to live on. Not a lot . . . but a few thousand to cover the increased costs of living with Julia . . . say five thousand at the most. That would leave twelve thousand for Stubbs. Not exactly all the money from the book, slightly under half; but Stubbs would *have* to understand this. I now realized this was something I hadn't thought about. It was all very philanthropic to offer him the money the way I did; but I should've thought about certain expenses that would inevitably have to come out of it before I could start offering anyone anything. 'Bloody fool', I said, reflecting regretfully now on my impetuousness.

"Ungrateful swine," I muttered, pre-supposing that Stubbs would query the amount. Okay, it's nothing compared to the money he lost, but if he really wanted to pick himself up, to make a new start, this must be some help, I decided, trying to assuage my troubled mind.

The erstwhile euphoria I experienced was now changing into gloomy introspection. A sense of foreboding hung over me. The way things were going, soon this dreaded meeting with Stubbs would have to take place. How was it possible to feel cheerful and optimistic with this hanging over my head? It's the conspiracy, that's what it is, I decided. This black cloud, this vile sinister ogre driven by evil spirits was determined to wreck any joy that it sensed: to snuff it out immediately; It knew when something good was about to happen, it couldn't stand watching anyone who was happy.

As I approached the coffee stall the tantalizing aroma of fried onions and freshly ground coffee tested all my powers of resistance. A few people were huddled around; some of the braver ones were sitting in the plastic chairs on the promenade pretending it was a beautiful summer's day. Knowing Julia would suggest the usual Welsh rarebit at The Copper Kettle, it would have been imprudent to stuff my face prior to our meeting. This little coffee stall for some reason provided a psychological demarcation point for my walk. As if by rote, I slowly did a circle around it enviously observing the succulent hot dogs being devoured, and started walking back.

By the time I'd made it back to my room there were still nearly two hours to kill before meeting Julia. It would take about twenty minutes to walk to her office so I sat in front of my typewriter hoping in the hour and a half that remained, to tap out a few more lines. For twenty minutes I sat there staring at a blank sheet of paper. It was no good, I just couldn't think. My agitation increased, I smoked several cigarettes, got up walked around the room and sat down again. Whatever was going to happen with Stubbs, I wanted it to happen now . . . quickly . . . get it over with. In my mind I could see him flying into an uncontrollable rage and half killing me when I mentioned the amount. Perhaps it might be easier to write out on a piece of paper the gross amount and then show the deductions that would reduce the amount he was to receive by more than half.

'Oh Christ', I thought, 'I'd have to stand next to him while he read it, watch his face contort . . . see the angry veins enlarge . . . and then' . . .'

'Oh God', the image conjured up by this was unbearable . . . far worse than any nightmare I'd ever had.

Julia of course, had no conception of just how terrified I was of him. The way I'd explained things to her was hardly in keeping with the grim reality of what faced me, or possibly both of us. I knew I should have told her from the start. The problem was that then we weren't together. Perhaps she did have an idea: I didn't make any attempt to disguise my fear that day in the stationers when she came up behind me and placed her hands over my eyes. How could I now bare my soul, reveal the truth? Of course it would be impossible. The whole ugly saga was now coming to an end. All I had to do was somehow keep it together for a few more days.

A broad smile covered Julia's face as she ran down the steps from her office to greet me.

"Tom I'm so excited for you its fantastic news," she said throwing her arms around me and kissing every part of my face.

"Yes, it still seems like a dream, I can't believe it."

"I always knew you'd do it, it's the best thing that's ever happened. Let's go over the road and grab a table before it gets too busy," she said looking over at The Copper Kettle.

I was finding it difficult to revive the elation I'd experienced earlier. Had I been able to share the news with her then: the very moment that I'd heard, it would've been different. Now with my mood having changed, it required an act for me to convey feelings that had since faded.

"What are you going to do about 'Mr Vince'; you're not still going to give him all that money surely?"

I had a careful look around the restaurant to make sure Stubbs hadn't followed us in and was lurking somewhere. That would've been all I needed.

"No, of course I'm not."

"What have you decided then?"

"Well," I said thoughtfully, "they're going to pay me twenty five thousand for the first book, and the same again for the second one. The second one is nothing to do with Stubbs; I offered to give him the money I got from the first one and that's it . . . and that's what he's going to get."

"Good God, you really are serious about this aren't you."

"Yes, the only thing is it won't be the twenty five grand that he's getting, there are various expenses that have to come out of it . . .like the agents fee, income tax and I'm going to keep a small amount back . . .you know . . .to live on for a bit. I did *write* the bloody thing after all."

My acting ability left much to be desired, a large crack had now appeared in my façade showing the bitterness and resentment that had been hovering beneath the surface.

There followed a strained embarrassed silence. Julia looked at me knowingly; she'd seen through me and I knew it.

"Well, what I mean is . . . I . . . I'd like to have given him the whole lot . . . but there it is."

"Gosh, under the circumstances I think he's bloody lucky to get anything. I mean you don't actually owe him a penny. I know you feel badly about what happened . . . but you were only doing your job. If it hadn't of been you, it would have been somebody else and I don't suppose they would be about to give him, a complete stranger, twelve grand. I mean he's dead lucky that you're such a softie."

"No, that's true I suppose. Right, what's it to be . . . No of course I don't need to ask," I said," putting the menu down. "Two of your delicious Welsh rarebit's and a pot of tea please," I reeled off as the spotty waitress approached.

"After you phoned, I spoke to the agents I rent my flat from; I asked them about a garden shed and you'd think I'd asked them if we could keep a gorilla there. 'No, no possibility whatsoever', they said, they couldn't even be bothered to ask the landlord."

"Oh well, thanks for trying. To be honest things have changed now. We could rent somewhere larger, or even buy somewhere . . . perhaps an old house."

"Oh yes that'd be amazing. The only thing is you've got to promise not to become pompous, you know flitting around in a cravat and a velvet smoking jacket reciting lines from poems all day; I couldn't stand that."

"I don't think there's much danger of that happening," I said, failing to appreciate the skittish vein of her humour. Had she really any idea of the reality of the task in hand? Clearly not judging from this glib comment.

"I do rather fancy acquiring a tortoise shell cigarette holder though to hold my black Russian Sobranie cigarettes. I might also invest a nice Victorian smoking cap with a silk tassel at some point."

This immediately produced guffaws of husky bronchitic laughter from Julia causing the whole restaurant to look over at her disapprovingly.

"Stop it," she said, "I'll get the giggles and we'll have to leave."

"Those were the days," I said mournfully as if I remembered them, "If you walked around here like that now you'd get your bloody head kicked in."

Something to do with her visual impression of this caused her to shriek with laughter; several more shrieks followed, the tears were running down her cheeks; the laughter was then terminated by a serious coughing fit.

I sensed that the spotty faced waitress was not enjoying our mirth as much as us, as she scowled and banged the two servings of Welsh rarebit down on the table. How dare anyone blatantly exhibit this unsanctimonious behaviour in The Copper Kettle!

"You mentioned having to go to London to meet your agent; Wednesday was it? Oh, I wish I could come with you."

"Yes, I do too, would you be able to take the day off?"

"I doubt it, but I'll ask my boss when I get back."

"Shall I phone you this evening to find out?"

"No better still," she said, "come round; we'll go out and eat somewhere . . .a celebration, I think is called for."

It seemed only a few moments ago that I'd been waiting on the steps outside her office to meet her and now I was back there kissing her goodbye.

"See you later," she shouted blowing a kiss to me as she disappeared through the large plate glass door into her office. I stood outside for a few moments collecting my thoughts. 'Better go back and do some work', I said to myself, and starting walking back towards my room. I was reflecting on the conversation we'd just had. The prospect of buying a house together was exciting. With the money coming in we could definitely afford it; even if Julia stopped working the monies coming in from my second book would keep us going for a while. Always at the back of my mind was the fact that Julia wanted to get married. Children would follow quickly enough; so we might as well plan ahead: or more succinctly, I might as well prepare myself for the inevitable.

I stopped and peered through an estate agents window at all the small Victorian houses on offer.

"Out house buying then?" A voice shouted from somewhere.

I jumped out of my skin, turned around and saw Clive grinning behind me.

"Good God, you frightened the life out of me."

"Its guilt, that's what it is; looking in the oppositions window."

"How are you? It's good to see you Clive, I was going to give you a ring, but things have been happening so quickly . . . I . . ."

"Don't worry, I've been busy myself. Have you come into some money then?" Clive said grinning.

"Well yes, something like that; I've finally got an offer for my book and Julia . . ."

"Oh that's brilliant news mate, don't tell me the two of you are getting married now and you're looking for a little nest."

"Oh Christ, I wish you wouldn't put it like that," I said, squirming at his description.

"Come on, don't be so worried, it happens to the best of us and let's face it Julia's a pretty good catch isn't she?"

"Yes of course she is. Don't mention the marriage thing at the moment though; I'm sure it'll happen quickly enough. It's just that I'm going to leave where I'm living at the moment and move back with Julia. Her flat, although it's nice, it's a bit like living in a shoe box really, so we thought about possibly buying somewhere together."

"No, I understand, what are you looking for a flat or a house?"

"Well, I don't really know, I mean a house would be terrific but I'm not sure if we could afford that at the moment."

"How much did they offer you for the book? If you don't mind me asking."

"Well for the first one it's twenty five grand with another twenty five for a sequel."

"Bloody hell: Congratulations mate, that's serious money. I thought you were talking about a few hundred pounds. And you're wondering if you can buy a house! Of course you can. Are you doing anything right now?"

"Hmm, I was going back to do some work. Why what have you got in mind?"

"I was just thinking that we could go back to my office, I'll get some keys and I can show you some of the properties we've got on our books. You might see something you fall in love with."

"Christ, you're always the salesman aren't you?"

"Don't be mad, it's just to give you an idea of what's around at the moment. With that sort of dosh I don't suppose you'll be needing a mortgage will you?"

"Oh yes, most definitely. It's not as much as it sounds after all the tax and commissions have been taken out of it. You have to remember that's money I need to live on, I don't get paid weekly or monthly like everyone else."

"No I understand what you're saying. In that case you'll need Duncan, Duncan Brown. Let's go back now and we can have a chat with him and see what he can do."

I'd taken an instant dislike to Duncan from the first time I'd set eyes upon him. His sickly ingratiating manner summarized everything I hated about commerce. Despite my obvious repugnance for him, I was nonetheless impressed by the suave confident way he approached his new victim. 'Ah a writer', he said, 'must be a nice way of earning a living'. It didn't take him long to confirm that we would have no trouble at all in getting a mortgage. Julia was earning about eight thousand a year and I could declare anything I liked on a self certification mortgage. All he had to do was make a quick call to the right people and the money would be available immediately for us.

Having sorted this out Clive picked up a few bunches of keys and he and I went out to view some properties. The first two that Clive showed me were very small Victorian terraced houses, both in need of modernisation and both of them on the market for twenty five thousand. The third one; much more interesting, was an early Victorian rectory just on the outskirts of the town. The property had two large ground floor rooms and a large kitchen, plus a smaller room at the back that would have made a perfect study. Upstairs there were four bedrooms and a bathroom. Although needing updating; all the existing period features were in tact and outside was a large overgrown west facing garden several outhouses and a large garage with an inspection pit. I was sold on it immediately.

"It's quite superb, how much is it?"

"It's only just come on the market; we're looking for offers in the region of forty thousand. It'll sell quickly: there aren't many of these left now, particularly n this position."

"I'd like Julia to see it. Perhaps tomorrow if that's okay with you I'll speak to her this evening."

That evening Julia was so excited by my positive action and my description of the house, she just couldn't wait until the next day to see it. Like a couple of naughty excited children we went over to the house and peered through the windows with a torch. At lunch time the next day Clive and I were sitting in a car outside Julia's office waiting to whisk her of to The Rectory the moment she surfaced.

An hour later, she was dropped back to work again after having issued explicit instructions that I must secure this house at any cost. She didn't really care how much it was, or how much work was needed; it was quite definitely love at first sight.

"Yes I'm happy to tell you I've got an offer of the full asking price," Clive said to the executors he was phoning, "The buyers have a mortgage agreed in principle and can proceed immediately. Right, thank you, we'll put the wheels in motion, and get the confirmation letters in the post today." I spent the best part of an hour filling forms in with Duncan providing the answers, and that was it. Clive agreed to drop the forms around to Julia for her details and signatures, and assured me that the deal was as good as done.

Sitting back in my room at Albion Mansions I was finding it difficult to fully comprehend the enormity of what had transpired in the last twenty four hours. The ambivalence I felt was a combination of excitement and trepidation. By some strange quirk of fate things were developing faster than I could keep pace with. Trying to focus my attention on writing was impossible. Perhaps after the meeting tomorrow things would get back to normal. I felt an unpleasant sinking feeling; a gnawing pain in the pit of my stomach. The five thousand pounds I was going to keep back to live on had now virtually been spent before I'd even seen a penny of it. Four thousand for the ten per cent deposit, legal fees, moving costs, yes this was now accounted for. Had I stayed on at Albion Mansions and continued to eek out the modest amount I'd saved, I could have just survived for another six months. Moving in with Julia and then shortly after that moving into The Rectory was rapidly going to exhaust my remaining funds. All my efforts now would have to be channelled into writing the sequel. Once I'd got tomorrow out of the way, that's what I'd do, I told myself sternly.

Julia's boss couldn't possibly spare her for the all important day . . .had she of asked him last week . . .if the office wasn't so busy etc, so I got the train up to see Jane Phillips by myself. I'd imagined some seductive femme fatale judging from the warm sensual voice on the telephone and was quite shocked when a plump middle aged woman with a crew cut appeared at the reception desk. For twenty minutes or so we sat in her office while she carefully explained how she imagined things would pan out. The contracts were signed and she promised to do everything she could to get the monies to me as quickly as possible. She had booked a table at a little Italian restaurant in the next road for one o'clock and with any luck Jeremy from the publishing house would be joining us as he was anxious to meet me as well.

Jeremy was an erudite sun tanned handsome fellow in his thirties who'd obviously benefited from a public school education. In this particular company I felt very much like a country bumpkin, having to think carefully about everything I said, terrified I might involuntarily say something which might make them have second thoughts about me.

Things did look very positive though; they both had great hopes for the first book and were equally enthusiastic about the second. If these sold well enough it could be the start of a promising career.

The train journey back seemed to last only a few minutes; I was preoccupied with the conversation we'd had in the restaurant and moreover with the unenviable prospect of facing Stubbs. Ever conscious of the fact that time was running out fast, I'd got to get this over with now; no more procrastinating. Julia had arranged to go to the cinema with Rachel this evening, some sickly romantic love story, I couldn't even remember the title of the film; this would be my chance. Once this had been taken care of I could relax again; get down to some serious writing.

Just after six o'clock I was back in my room. I ran through the speech I'd rehearsed again and then knocked loudly on Stubbs's door. The door opened almost immediately, he didn't say anything, just stared at me aggressively.

"I wonder if I might have a word with you," I said.
He said nothing. He continued to stare at me for a further five seconds, opened the door wider and stood aside to allow me into the room.

"It's about the book," I said with a catch in my voice.
"What about the book?"

"Well, I've had an offer for it . . . that's what I wanted to talk to you about."

"Hmm, how much is it?"

"Well the gross amount is twenty five grand, but . . ."

"I suppose that'll have to do won't it?"

"Look it's not exactly that straight forward, that's what I . . ."

"Sounds straight forward enough to me, if it's twenty five grand just give me the fucking money and piss off. Nothing complicated about that."

"Please listen," I pleaded with him already feeling exasperated by this aggressive stance but also fearing the worst.

"The net amount I can give you won't be that. There are certain deductions that have to be made. There is the agent's commission, income tax, and I need something to live on myself. I'm trying to be as fair as I . . ."

"Oh I see," he said, "I understand. I expected this. Once you got the money I knew you'd try and worm your way out of it. You forget I'm old in the tooth, my little writer friend; there's not much you can tel me about human nature. Come on then: tell me, what has your scheming devious little mind come up with now?"

"Look, I'm being totally straight with you; I'm just trying to explain that the amount I can give you won't be twenty five thousand. It's going to be more like twelve thousand. With any luck I will have the money in the next week or . . ."

"Where's the letter you got from these people . . . with the offer set out? Come on show me."

"I haven't got a letter yet. I've only just heard from them myself. I went up to London to meet them today. I've come straight back here because I wanted to keep to my word and tell you straight away."

"To tell me straight away eh? . . . To tell me you're only going to give me half the fucking money. And you call that keeping to your word do you? You've cost me nearly half a million quid with your petty devious scheming and you think I should be happy with twelve paltry grand . . . that I should get down on my bended knees and kiss your feet . . .you fucking nasty little shit."

"I'm sorry," I said without thinking, "I was hoping you'd understand."

"Understand? Understand? What I do understand you little shit is that you've wrecked my life and you think twelve measly grand is going to compensate me for that?"

"I can't give you money I haven't got. I desperately need the money myself but I'm trying to show you that I really am sorry for what happened."

"And so you fucking should be."

I paused for a moment trying to work out whether he was going to accept this before divulging further potentially dangerous revelations.

"The other thing is I shall be moving out of here soon."

"Oh I see, so you think you've got rid of me for twelve grand and now you're off to live the high life somewhere where I can't keep an eye on you, yeah I've got it. Moving in with Julia are you?"

I tried to avoid looking at him aware that he was whipping himself up for some sort of frenzied attack.

"I'm buggered if I know what a woman like that sees in a pathetic little worm like you."

I ignored this and backed towards the door. "I'll be leaving here at the end of the month," I said. "If the money isn't through by then I'll bring it around here to you as soon as it arrives. Do you want cash or is a cheque okay?"

"Bring it in cash."

"Okay I will. There is just one thing you must understand though."

"Tell me what it is 'I must understand'? You little wretch."

"If Julia sees you anywhere near her flat she'll call the police. There'd be nothing I could do to stop her. If that happens . . ."

"Don't threaten me, whatever you do don't try to threaten me . . ." he said clipping each word. "I'm warning you, I will kill the fucking pair of you. Now if you've said what you came here to say, I've got better things to do than listen to your squealing."

Chapter 8

What an emotional time it was when I moved out of Albion Mansions! Mrs Hoskins tried her best to fight back the tears at the thought of losing 'their young writer', or perhaps it was just the seventy five pounds a week. Even Jack managed to emit a few soulful grunts at the prospect of me leaving. It didn't take long for Clive and I to bag up my few moth eaten clothes and other bits and pieces and load them into Clive's car which was double parked outside. I insisted on carrying what Julia had described as my beloved prehistoric typewriter down myself, which was carefully placed on the back seat.

"Be glad to get out of here won't you?" Clive shouted through a bundle of clothes he was lugging down the staircase.

"No, sad really . . . if anything." I said.

"Well at least you can look back on it in the future. Maybe they'll put one of those blue plaques up outside."

"Steady on," I said, "I think you've got to be dead before that happens."

An officious looking traffic warden was waiting alongside the car when we came out of the building with his book open and a pen in his hand.

"Hang on mate, we're just moving somebody out of this building," Clive pleaded, "two minutes and we'll be gone."

"Is this a commercial vehicle?" The warden asked sarcastically.

"No it's not, but I had to stop to load up all of this," he said pointing to what looked like a pile of rags falling out of black plastic sack on the pavement.

"Right move it right now or I'll write out a ticket."

"Yes, yes of course," Clive responded, "thanks for being so understanding,"

"Bastard," he shouted out the window as we drove off. "I hope he dies slowly of something extremely painful."

In less than ten minutes we were outside Julia's flat. Within five minutes what had hitherto been an attractive little flat had now been transformed into something resembling a refugee camp.

"Right, good luck mate, I'll leave you to it, I must get back to the office now I've got three viewings lined up. And oh, if you and Julia are still together this evening give me a ring and we'll go out for a drink," he said with a wry smile.

I stood for a few moments staring at all the split plastic bags lined up all over the floor wondering if I should make an effort to put things away somewhere. I opened a wardrobe in the bedroom which was packed tightly with Julia's clothes. A quick look in the chests of drawers revealed the same. I was beginning to feel uneasy. I could just picture Julia's face when she came in from work: the comments she would make were already resonating through my head. 'Good God, I didn't realise you had so much stuff', she would say. 'I don't know where we can put it all'. At least two of the disintegrating plastic bags contained dubious items of clothing that were well overdue for the launderette. Because other matters had taken precedence I'd not got round to dealing with this. Perhaps this might be an ideal opportunity to run them through her washing machine; at least all the clean clothes could then be stacked up neatly somewhere which would provide proof if any was needed, of my desire to conform to some form of domestic normality.

The washing machine though presented a serious challenge. I looked around for the instructions which she must have hidden away somewhere. I'd mastered the controls of the launderette machines but this was much more complicated. After a frantic search through all the kitchen cupboards and drawers, having pulled most of their contents out on to the floor, I decided to *just* give it a try.

After stuffing the machine as tightly as I could and filling up all the powder trays to the brim, I forced the door shut and started twisting, turning and pulling all the knobs on the front of the machine. Things were now looking quite promising; a red light came on together with the sound of water entering the machine. 'Not so difficult after all', I muttered and returned to the lounge to unpack and prepare the next load.

Having unloaded the second bag, I piled the soiled clothes up outside the kitchen door to await their turn. The next vital operation was to find somewhere to place my typewriter. A quick evaluation of the likely places pointed to the little stripped pine desk in front of the bay window. I cleared away the photograph frames and other knick knacks and lovingly positioned it there. Unfortunately in the move, the little rubber feet at the bottom of it had come off and as I slid it into position it made four deep gouges across the top of the desk.

'Bugger', I said bitterly, knowing how much she treasured this piece of furniture.

The little wooden chair in front of the desk was extremely uncomfortable and was far too low. A few cushions eventually brought it up to what seemed a decent height; it was now just a matter of placing some paper in the machine and giving it a try. Yes, this was fine! I tapped away for half an hour or so, happy in the knowledge that I'd found somewhere to work. The last time I'd lived here my typewriter was on the coffee table and that was most unsatisfactory. After a couple of hours I'd end up with the most crucifying back ache. This was much better. I started tapping away trying to get used to my new environment. Pausing to think about the next paragraph, I heard some strange noises coming from the kitchen. I turned around and to my horror saw a large wave of glistening bubbles seeping under the door into the lounge. I stared at it for a few moments in disbelief; 'what on earth . . .' I got up and warily walked over to the kitchen door, opened it and gasped. The whole kitchen had been invaded by some giant foaming monster creeping and rising by the second. I ran through it towards the machine and tried to turn it off. Nothing happened; the red light stayed on and the foam continued to pour out. In my panic and desperation, I tugged at the door; but it wouldn't seem to open. 'This can't be happening', I said to myself giving it a further violent tug, at which the door flew open and the water and foam inside cascaded across the kitchen.

It didn't take long for the woman in the flat below to appear in the garden and shout up to me, "Hey, what's going on up there? My kitchen's flooded; there's water pouring through the ceiling."

I opened the window and peered down into the garden to see where the shouting was coming from.

"Oh I'm sorry there's been a slight accident," I said.

"Who are you?" she shrieked. "What are you doing in there? Doe's 'the young lady know you're in there?"

I now desperately wanted to escape. To be back in the comparative safety of Albion Mansions. 'It's the conspiracy; that's what's doing it', I said to myself. 'It's pointless trying to fight it; it's determined to do its evil job'.

When Julia returned at lunch time to see how I was settling in; the atmosphere was electric; the language was blue. After stating unequivocally that I was an incompetent ham fisted buffoon; things seemed to go from one crisis to another.

After the first week, although our relationship was on a knife edge, a sense of calm did eventually prevail. The fact that our proposed purchase of The Rectory was still on course, no doubt contributed to Julia's determination to survive this frustratingly aggravating episode. I could see clearly now why our relationship hit the rocks before. Apart from Julia's domineering personality, we were living on top of each other which didn't help. It was absolutely imperative to have some space. Living in this confined space and trying to write . . . no it simply couldn't be done.

Our spirits were instantly and magically revitalized by the letter I received a few days later from Jane Phillips containing a cheque for twenty one thousand, five hundred and ninety three pounds and seventy five pence. We waved it around, jumped up and down and celebrated with a bottle of champagne which Julia had kept at the back of the fridge especially for this occasion. The woman in the flat below though didn't share our joy; now couldn't wait for us to move.

Three days after paying the cheque in, I presented the cashier at the bank with a cheque made out to cash for twelve thousand pounds. After an inordinate delay, a lot of whispering and a host of eyes behind the counter staring at me suspiciously, a weasel faced bank manager appeared and asked if he might have a word.

"I don't think I've had the pleasure . . ." he said ushering me into his office.

"No, I agreed."

"I hope you understand it's really for security reasons; this is quite a substantial sum of money . . ."

"Yes."

"Now let me just have a look at the account." (The ledger was open on his desk which he'd clearly already looked at), ah yes, I see you deposited a considerable sum with the bank three days ago. May I ask is this from a property transaction?"

"No."

"Well it would help us to know a little more . . . there are many services the bank can offer clients such as yourself investment advice, insurance, you know a whole range of services to . . . you know . . . shall we say for substantial depositors like yourself."

"I am sure, but I don't need any of this thank you."

"No, no that's perfectly alright . . . it's just that . . . well it is rather a large . . ."

165

"Okay, I'm a writer. The money is from my agent, it's an advance on a book."

"Oh a writer indeed, now that *is* interesting. What sort of books do you write?"

"Look I don't wish to be rude but I'm in a hurry. Could I please have the money?"

"Oh yes of course, do forgive me it'll just be a few moments, I'll get the cashier to get it from the safe for you. Any particular denominations you'd like for the notes sir?"

"Fifties will do fine thanks."

I tried unsuccessfully to appear nonchalant when a few minutes later the bank manager counted out the tightly bound packages in front of me.

". . . eight, nine, ten, eleven, twelve . . . there we are sir, would you like to check it with me again?"

"No that's fine, there's no need."

Gazing at the pile of money sitting in front of me, I was momentarily overcome with a truculent inofficiousness, thinking of how much we needed this money to make our new house habitable. 'Oh well, no going back now', I thought, and stuffed the packages of notes into a crumpled plastic bag I produced from my pocket.

"If there's anything else we can . . ."

"No, that's it for the moment, and thanks for your . . ."

"Oh it's my pleasure . . . anytime."

'Right; don't think about it . . . just go round and give him the money', I thought, as I started walking in the direction of Albert Mansions. Having dispelled any ridiculous last minute notions of keeping the money, I now wanted to get rid of it as quickly as possible and try and erase the whole unpleasant episode from my memory.

With a positive determination I climbed the ten flights of stairs up to the top floor and stood breathless outside my old room. After pausing for a few moments to compose myself I knocked on Stubbs's door. There was no answer. Visibly trembling and with my heart pounding, I knocked again more loudly. Suddenly the door sprung open and Stubbs appeared like some terrifying lunatic: unshaven, bleary eyed and with a noticeable bruise and a cut on the left side of his forehead.

"What are you after?" he said menacingly.
I now felt more frightened than ever. Something had happened . . . a fight . . . God knows.

"It's the money," I said holding the bag out in front of me.

"Come in."
I cautiously stepped inside and was almost overccme by the vile fetid atmosphere. Stubbs closed the door and ominously locked it from the inside. A spine chilling pause followed with him standing no more than a foot away from me breathing stale alcohol fumes into my face.

" . . . It's the twelve thousand as agreed," I said handing him the bag. "Do you want to check it?"

"No give it here," he demanded.
He snatched the bag from me and violently threw it across the room over onto the bed. "You think you're doing me a favour don't you? You pathetic little creep."

"Well no, not exactly. I thought we'd . . ."

"Yeah, I know you thought that would wipe the slate clean," he said pointing his head towards the plastic bag on the bed. "You thought twelve fucking grand would make amends for all the damage you've caused. You thought I'd kiss your bloody feet for being so magnanimous. I know exactly what you thought you little shit. Twelve paltry grand is a drop in the ocean compared with what you've taken away from me. Do you think I like living here in this filth?" He grabbed me by the lapels and shook me. The expanded vein on the left side of his head appeared to be breaking through the bruised skin. "You fucking little shit . . ."

"Look . . . look please . . ."

"Yeah I've been waiting to see your smug little face thinking you've bought me off, while you bugger off and start living the high life spending all the money you're about to make with that painted bint of yours while I stay here and rot."

"Vince, please," I pleaded shaking with fear, "I can't undo what's happened. I've explained how sorry . . ."

"Don't fucking 'Vince' me you loathsome little worm. Get out of here now before I do what I should've done the moment I caught up with you."

Realising his grip on me, he leant forward and unlocked the door, opened it, put his angry contorted face a few inches away from mine and spat into it. I staggered out onto the landing wiping the spittle away from my face with the back of my hand as the door was slammed shut with the sound of the lock being turned.

My legs were giving way with fear as I attempted to sedately negotiate the stairs down to the ground floor. I kept looking back up the staircase imagining that Stubbs might have come out again after me. This hadn't gone at all according to plan. I couldn't believe what had just transpired. Of course I didn't in all honesty expect Stubbs to be pleasant but . . . There was no doubt this man was mad; completely deranged, highly unpredictable and most certainly dangerous. He didn't even check the money. There could have been bundles of newspaper in the bag. The fact that I'd just given him twelve thousand pounds hadn't made a single jot of difference.

The more I dwelt on it as I strolled back to Julia's flat, the more annoyed and frustrated I felt. A corrosive despair was eating into me. Was this going to be the end of the matter? If not, if Stubbs started to reappear again outside Julia's flat I would *have* to go to the police; Julia would insist on it. That would in the end, make matters far worse for both of us: it would also then suggest that giving him the twelve thousand pounds would have been completely pointless. This would be an extremely bitter pill to swallow knowing how much we both needed the money just to make our new house habitable.

What a hollow victory this had turned out to be. I didn't expect a pat on the back from Stubbs; of course not. I had imagined that at least some sort of accord might have been reached. I had after all honoured my word. I'd turned up without any prompting with the money . . . and to be treated like this . . . In my mind I'd gone through it on numerous occasions: I'd hand Stubbs the money: Stubbs would be pleasantly surprised that I'd kept to my word: we'd both agree to put the past behind us, shake hands and that would be the end of the matter. Julia would be bound to say 'I bet he was pleased when you showed up unexpectedly with a bag full of money': how could I tell her what happened? She'd be as devastated as I was. 'Oh what a bloody awful life it is after all', I muttered to myself. 'It's the conspiracy that's what it is. It doesn't matter what you try to do, it'll poke its malignant little nose in at some point and sabotage it for you. Yes that's one thing you can depend upon'.

For some indefinable reason I found it extraordinarily difficult to write at Julia's flat. I spent many hours sitting at her little desk day dreaming. During moments of comparative lucidity I tried to analyze why this was so. Certainly the change of surroundings was a contributing factor but not solely the problem. The wretched business with Stubbs was still playing heavily on my mind, as was our imminent move to The Rectory. I loved the character of the place; the very idea of living there with Julia being able to follow my dream of writing and with not only her approval but her encouragement as well. My next book was as good as sold with a further not insubstantial amount of money due to me on completion. This really was everything I could have ever have hoped for.

What then was the problem? My mind was playing tricks on me, leading me down blind ally's; attributing the cause of my creative absence and lethargy to any number of unspecific extraneous explanations all of which were devoid of substance. Many days passed where Julia would go off to work and I would sit in front of my typewriter as if in a trance staring out of the window. The truth of the matter was something I couldn't bear to face. When initially I offered Stubbs the money, it was because I was being attacked. I feared for my life. The money was offered to Stubbs in desperation to stop a further violent assault that was about to be unleashed. I genuinely thought I was about to be murdered. Yes I did feel a certain sympathy for Stubbs and the callous way the claim had been dealt with, but I no doubt would have shrugged that off; after all many claims were rejected in this way, not just by me, or the company I worked for; but by every insurance company in business.

No, the truth which was now haunting me and not infrequently staring me in the face wasn't some nebulous mystical phenomena: it was the fact that I was undeniably a coward. I was trying desperately not to have to admit it; but this was the problem. At school I'd always shied away from any conflict, I was not only shy and timid; I was terrified of other bigger boys that would taunt and ridicule me over any number of my inadequacies. The thought of physical violence in any form was abhorrent. I'd tried in vain to convince not only myself, but Julia as well, that giving Stubbs the money we so urgently needed was out of compassion and nothing else.

It was undoubtedly the unsatisfactory outcome of my last humiliating encounter with Stubbs that was perniciously teasing my subconscious. I'd handed the money over on the misguided assumption that Stubbs would have allowed me to maintain this self deception. The fact that Stubbs had ungratefully snatched the money from me and then literally spat in my face was the empirical proof if any were needed of my cowardice.

Worse still I wondered if Julia had suspected this all along. My pretence at being so conscience driven and charitable was probably glaringly incongruous, even to Julia.

Yes this was what was troubling me. One way or another I'd have to try and put it behind me. Only Julia would ever know about it and there was always the possibility that I'd evaluated the situation with disproportionate pessimism.

Although unpalatable as it was, I did over the next few weeks come to terms with the unpleasant reality of the situation; however there were still serious uncertainties lingering as to what the future held. The peace of mind I craved was an elusive and reluctant accomplice. The thing I now feared most was to find Stubbs lurking outside or even worse. For many nights now I'd been troubled by the same horrific nightmare: of waking up and seeing Stubbs standing over both of us wielding a long bloodstained knife above his head. I could see clearly the veins bursting out of his forehead and a scathing murderous expression on his face as he brought the knife down into our flesh.

I daren't have told Julia about these nightmares despite the fact that on the last two occasions when I'd woken up shouting in a fit of terror with perspiration running down my face, she must have realized something was amiss with me. 'Just a bad dream', I would say, get up and go into the kitchen to make tea, I'd then sit there for another hour smoking while she would go back to sleep. In the morning she'd ask me what the dream was about and every time I had to invent something new.

The good news was that we had our mortgage offer approved; we'd signed the contract on The Rectory and in less than four weeks we would be moving in. To a certain extent the knowledge of this provided the impetus I needed to press on with my writing. The other reassuring aspect of this was that in four weeks Stubbs could hang around outside the flat as much as he wanted. No one in the road knew us, or would have any idea of where we'd moved to.

One thing was certain though; having been through our now depleted finances, we agreed that we'd have to live in The Rectory as it was until money was forthcoming from the second book. We were both excited at the prospect of actually living there and were unconcerned that we'd have to rough it until then. We reassured each other that by mid March, the time we would move in; the weather would be warmer and central heating wouldn't be necessary. The fact that the electricity had been cut off as the wiring and the old round pin fifteen amp power sockets were dangerous, was a detail: as was the leak in the roof. The antiquated plumbing was nothing to worry about either. I had no doubt that once the coal had been removed from the enormous cast iron bath at the back of the scullery it would clean up and be as good as new!

As the days grew closer our laissez faire gung ho attitude, the disregard for modern amenities, came into question as the skies became darker, the weather got noticeably colder, and flurries of snow appeared. Julia's flat might have been cramped; but at least it was warm and comfortable. With now just five days to go before the move we both felt a sense of foreboding.

"I'm sure it'll be fine once we've settled in," Julia stated positively.

"Oh yes, I'm sure it will be a bit strange at first . . . all that space and . . ."

"Perhaps we ought to buy a few cheap electric convector heaters if it's going to be this cold next week," she said.

"Nice idea," I agreed, "trouble is there's nowhere to plug them in. We won't have any electricity until we get the place rewired."

"Oh God yes, I'm just wondering . . . do you think we're being silly? I mean do you think we're doing the right thing?"

"Of course. Well it's too late now to worry about it." I said looking extremely *worried.* "Even if they allowed us to stay on here, we can't afford to pay for two properties can we? Anyway we won't have any money to carry out any work on it until I get the next advance from the publishers, and that could be another six months yet. Sure things might be a bit difficult initially, but we've got to look at it in the long term."

"Oh I think actually it'll be quite romantic. We've got the hurricane lamps and candles for lighting; we could get one of those Calor gas heaters if it's still really cold. If the old kitchen range is cleaned out . . . Clive said that it probably heats the hot water so we can use all that coal in the bath and burn it in that. It's going to be fun trying to cook on top of it . . . we'll be living the way our ancestors did."

"Yes it will be fun . . . or at least interesting even," I said unconvincingly.

On the day of the move the temperature dropped, the sky darkened, the wind got up and then torrential rain fell from the sky. In order to preserve our meagre funds I'd hired 'a man with a van' to move Julia's furniture and our general belongings. Both Julia and I were afflicted with head banging hangovers; the regrettable aftermath of a night celebrating our completion of the purchase with Clive and Rachel.

As paid the driver, Julia stood in the bitterly cold hallway watching the water cascading down through the missing guttering by the open front door.

She pushed the door to in an effort to stop a further deluge as it bounced on the quarry tiled floor cf the porch and into the hall. The sound of a minor waterfall somewhere else demanded her attention. Following the sound of the water falling, her faced drcpped dramatically as she found a constant trickle of water pouring out of the light fitting in the kitchen ceiling which was falling into an old galvanized bath that had been strategically placed on the floor underneath it. When I returned like a drowned rat I found Julia in tears in the kitchen.

"This is ridiculous," she whimpered, "we can't stay here, we shouldn't have bought this place, we've got nowhere to go, what are we going to do?

Realizing the urgency of the situation I came up with the perfect solution. I ran upstairs and placed an old bucket at the point where it was coming through the ceiling above.

"That'll stop it getting into the kitchen," I said buoyantly. "It's probably only a slate or two missing from

the roof. All we have to do is remember to empty it . . .
I'll keep an eye on it."

Eventually the rain eased off: After several failed
attempts I finally managed to get some coal burning in
the old kitchen range which provided a modicum of
cheer to the dismal surroundings. After some serious
gurgling, bangs, and clonks and finally some
strangulated spluttering noises; some warm dark brown
water appeared from the kitchen tap.

I couldn't contain my excitement: I shouted up to
Julia who was upstairs trying to make up a bed for us,
"hot water! . . . It works . . . we've got hot water!"
Julia flew down the stairs overjoyed at this latest
revelation, the expression then quickly changed to one
of horror when she saw the gush of filthy brown water
coming out of the tap depositing disturbing looking black
specs over the sink.

"Ooh you must be crazy, that's disgusting: I'm not
bathing in that . . . If we get that on us we'll end up with
all sorts of terrible diseases."

"Wait!" I shouted, unable to contain my excitement,
"it's clearing . . . it's just the rust in the old pipes."

After a few minutes the water became crystal clear
and piping hot as clouds of steam rose up to the ceiling.
The next task awaiting me was to remove several
hundred weight of coal from the bath to one of the
dilapidated outhouses. Now with copious supplies of hot
water Julia set about cleaning the kitchen. The old
cream enamel sink top was scrubbed vigorously as was
the old three legged pine kitchen table that had been left
by the previous occupants.   As the light faded we
lighted two of the hurricane lamps we'd bought and a

few candles. At least now our initial despair was passing . . . some positive moves were underway . . . Things could only get better now!

The next day, with Clive's assistance a local builder was employed to patch up the roof as a temporary measure, after which he informed me gloomily that the whole thing was 'shot'. He also agreed to let us have estimates for rewiring, re-plumbing, installing central heating and numerous other repairs. When the estimates arrived; I winced on seeing the total cost of all these items was just a few pennies under twelve thousand pounds. This would certainly give Julia cause to question my sanity in having given this amount to Stubbs 'because I felt sorry for him'.

For the past few weeks my writing had virtually been put on hold. This was causing me immense frustration. Although Julia and I were slowly beginning to enjoy the benefits of The Rectory, it was now the beginning of April: I had completed only about a third of my second book and knew time was running out. We urgently needed the money from it to have the work carried out on the house before the winter set in. The weather now was improving, the days longer and although it was still chilly inside the house, it was just bearable. Neither of us despite our initial bravado could contemplate a full English winter in such circumstances.

The problem was that every day, Julia produced a never ending list of jobs that had to be carried out before I could sit down and write. When finally, my frustration reached fever pitch a compromise between us was reached. By starting work as soon as Julia left in the morning I would work on the house until lunch time carrying out a multitude of different tasks and would then concentrate on writing in the afternoon. This would allow me at least four hours a day to continue with the book.

Theoretically this should have worked, but in practice it didn't: when I did finally sit down to write my brain was being bombarded with outstanding problems, things that needed cleaning or repairing; it was destroying my creative train of thought. By the end of the month I'd only completed another chapter. Now a further degree of mutual understanding was required. The way things were going; the book simply wouldn't be finished. I needed to work at it full time, five whole days a week. We could *both* spend the weekends doing things to the house . . . that was the only solution. Once the book was finished and the cheque paid over to me we'd have time to breathe. Julia obviously sensed my frustration and agreed. After this, things more or less got back on an even keel.

Towards the end of June everything was going according to plan; the book was now nearing completion: we'd cleared the enormous overgrown garden and had decorated two of the ground floor rooms and our bedroom upstairs. It was a beautiful summer's morning; Julia had just left to go to work and I was making myself some tea before settling down in front of my typewriter, when there was a loud knock on the front door. As The Rectory was at the end of an unmade road and virtually off the beaten track, we hadn't really been troubled by salesmen or canvassers since we'd moved in. I jumped spilling my mug of scalding tea over my hand and went to the door cursing.

What I saw when I opened it took me completely by surprise: There standing outside holding a bottle of champagne, was Stubbs.

"I thought I might find you in," he said.

My heart almost stopped beating: I couldn't speak, I stood there petrified.

"I just wanted to congratulate you."

"What do you mean?" I replied with a noticeable catch in my voice.

"I've just heard the good news."

"What do you mean?" I asked.

"Here . . . It's in the paper . . ." he replied handing me the folded paper with an article encircled in red ink.

I warily took the newspaper from him and read the article.

'£50,000 FOR DUBUT AUTHOR'
'First time writer Tom Dunford is paid £50,000, for a two book deal. His first book 'One Murder too Many', shortly to be released, is to be followed by a sequel by the end of the year. Tom Dunford etc,'

"I'm probably not the first, but when I saw that I just had to say how pleased I am for you, and to prove it I bought this (he said, holding out the bottle of champagne) on my way over to you. Now this really does call for a little celebration don't you think . . . just you and I? Just the two of us eh?"

"Look . . . I . . . I don't wish to be rude but I thought . . . I thought we'd concluded this business . . . you know I thought . . ."

"*And so did I*," Stubbs replied emphatically. "Now aren't you going to invite me in?"

"Yes," I said without thinking. Something told me that I didn't have a choice in the matter. Stubbs would have pushed passed me into the house anyway.

Stubbs followed me into the kitchen, placed the bottle on the draining board and turned his head slowly to take in the surroundings.

"Very impressive," he said, "very nice. Must have cost a pretty penny all of this?"

"It was cheap because there's a lot of work needed," I replied: annoyed with myself for responding.

"Well I'll open this," he said lifting up the bottle of champagne, "perhaps you can find us a couple of glasses."

I was desperately trying to think of a way of curtailing this little social encounter; suspecting with suppressed terror what was about to follow, but my brain had been anaesthetized with shock and fear. I just wanted Stubbs to go. Without saying anything I placed two glasses on the three legged kitchen table and tried to avoid looking into the face of Stubbs.

'Pop', went the cork as the frothing liquid streamed down the bottle and on to the floor. Stubbs filled a glass, placed it in mys shaking hand and then filled his own.

"Here's to our good fortune," he said putting the glass to his mouth. "Every cloud has a silver lining."

"Cheers," I said pathetically, hoping this charade would end soon, but at the same time dreading what was to come.

"Now, in the light of this 'error of judgement' being exposed, I think perhaps we need to have a little chat don't you?"

"What error of judgement? What do you mean?"

"Well I think both of us understand what I'm eluding to don't you?"

"No, I don't think so," I replied, finding it difficult now to even speak.

"I'm surprised at you then. I thought you were more intelligent. Or perhaps you're just playing games with me, is that it? Well, as your brain doesn't seem to be functioning clearly this morning, let me put it to you in simple terms. Being an extremely reasonable fellow that I think you must agree I am . . ."

Stubbs paused as if waiting for conformation on this point.

" . . .Well anyway, being a reasonable fellow, one that's always prepared to make allowances for the shortcomings of others, I believed you when you told me about the twenty five grand that you were getting for the book. I also believed . . ."

"Stop, just a minute, wait I . . ."

"No. You fucking wait you little shit. Not only have you prevented me from having the money that was rightfully mine five years ago: you are now trying to cheat me out of money I gracefully accepted as compensation from you. Now as I say, I'm a very reasonable man: I hate any form of violence but . . .'

"Look," I tried to get the words out. I . . ."

"Don't worry," Stubbs replied reassuringly, "as I say, I hate violence and I sure you'll agree it's not really going to be the best way to resolve this little oversight that's unfortunately occurred. The simple fact of the matter is that you owe me thirteen grand. I'm not asking for it today, although if I weren't reasonable . . . No I'm prepared to wait until your next payment arrives. Now how's that for being reasonable? Cheers."

"This is unbelievable," I said almost to myself in disbelief. "This really isn't fair. I promised you the money from my book and that's exactly what I've given you. The first book I got twenty five thousand for and after deductions that allowed me to give you twelve. I thought you understood that."

"The deal my friend, that you've secured . . . is for fifty . . . look (he picked up the newspaper and held it up); any deductions can come out of your part. I want the *full* amount that you offered me is that clear?"

"Yes . . . but . . ."

"Yes but nothing. Now this is supposed to be a happy celebration: let's not ruin it eh? When do you expect the rest of the money? I'm reasonable as I keep saying, but I don't propose to wait too long."

"The book should be finished in a month to six weeks I guess."

"Right, *now* we seem to understand one another. I'll give you until the end of August; now what could be more reasonable than that?"

"Look I . . . Okay, okay now if you don't mind I have work to do." I replied desperate to get him out of the house at any cost.

"Of course," Stubbs replied: "and congratulations once again!"

Chapter 9

I closed the front door and bolted it top and bottom. With my back against it I slid down onto the floor and sat with my head between my knees and both hands pressed over my face. My world had collapsed. I was now going through the worst nightmare I could have possibly imagined. Now everything was lost. All my hopes; all my dreams; the future . . . all of it destroyed. This was the lowest point I'd ever reached: I felt suicidal; there was no way out.

An icy shiver ran down my spine when I thought about what had just happened. How did he know where we'd moved to? How did he know that Julia wasn't at home? Before knocking on the door he must have been hiding somewhere near the house, watching; waiting for her to go off to work; choosing the right time to call.

The same old arguments presented themselves. Should I now go to the police? Should Julia be told about this visit and the latest demand? There *were* no answers. I'd been through it before so many times; my brain was weary at having to reconsider this unpleasantly familiar conundrum.

One thing was certain: this time, if I told Julia, she would immediately tell the police out of pure anger, if nothing else. Julia though, had no idea what he was like or what he might be capable of. The problem was as before; no doubt they would interview him . . . it's possible they might even arrest him . . . no not really . . . what would they arrest him for . . . what charge? The money that I'd been paid him was in cash . . . there would be no record of this: no proof. The visit today; Stubbs would maintain was a social call. No . . . all that going to the police would achieve would be to antagonise him making him even more vengeful. But this demand was quite ridiculous; we urgently needed the next payment due from the sequel; every penny of it was of paramount importance. Something *has* to be done, I kept telling myself again and again.

Any attempt now at writing today was just a forlorn hope. The incentive to finish the book had suddenly evaporated. What was the point now?

I dragged myself up and walked into the kitchen. I picked up the champagne bottle standing on the table it was still half full. In a trance like state I poured it down the sink momentarily fascinated by the vibrant singing and dancing of the frothy liquid as it disappeared down the waste hole; a last resounding gurgle and it was gone. I then dropped the empty bottle and the cork into the waste bin. Ten seconds later I pulled it out again. Julia would ask what it was doing there. I hadn't decided what to tell her yet but why complicate matters? I opened the back door, grabbed a spade from the outhouse and buried it at the bottom of the garden. 'That's one thing dealt with' I told myself.

The next forty five minutes were spent smoking cigarettes whilst pacing up and down the hallway racking my brains for some sort of solution. Maybe . . . just possibly, I might tell Julia. If I did tell her, she would be bound to ask where the empty bottle was. Having thought about this I went back into the garden and dug it up; took it into the kitchen and washed it carefully before placing it back in the bin. I cleaned the cork and put on top of it. Was I now unwittingly creating a precedent? Was this a decision made by my sub conscious mind to tell her the truth? Perhaps I was going mad. Perhaps Stubbs had now tipped me over the edge. I wasn't acting rationally. This was the behaviour of an insane person. No, for the moment the bottle had to go. I picked it out of the bin again and hid it in the outhouse. Julia would never go in there she was terrified of spiders. 'Right, now my options are open again', I muttered, feeling relieved as if some form of resolution had finally been reached over the more serious problem that faced us.

After another half an hour of pacing up and down I sat at my desk and tried to devise a logical plan to deal with this. As things stood . . . the facts of the case; there was very little the police would do other than probably make things worse. If I provoked him into attacking me (which would hardly be difficult); provided I survived the attack and was physically injured in some way, the police would almost certainly charge him with something. Very likely this would be assault, actual bodily harm, grievous bodily harm . . . something like this. If it was really serious it might be malicious wounding or even (my blood ran cold) attempted murder.

Assuming for the sake of argument it was some kind of vicious assault where I sustained just a few cuts and bruises and nothing more serious; at best, Stubbs; depending upon whether he had any previous convictions, might get sent to prison for a year, maybe eighteen months, or possibly even two or three years.

He'd be released after having served half of the sentence and would then be more dangerous than ever. No, this wasn't the answer. Something more radical was required.

The prospect of giving him the money we desperately needed was ludicrous. Even if I agreed, Julia certainly wouldn't, and if I were to try and dig my heels in, it would certainly mean the end of our relationship.

Thirteen thousand pounds was the sum he was demanding. For less than half this amount a contract killer could be hired. Yes . . . that puts things in proportion I said to myself. The only slight problem with this though, was how to find one. The diamond glint of madness flashed across my eyes as I laughed manically at the idea of looking through Yellow Pages under 'K' for killers or 'H' for hit men. I then considered the possibility of placing a small ad' for suitable candidates in the local paper under 'situations vacant'; which brought about further shrieks of insane laughter.

By lunch time an element of pragmatism came to the fore. Two things were indisputable: the book was a priority; it must be completed as quickly as possible. Stubbs had given me until the end of August. The sooner this was completed, the more time I would have to decide on a course of action. The second; was that he'd not get another penny from us: come what may . . . that much I had decided.

Despite this positive reasoning, I spent the remainder of the afternoon staring vacantly at the blank sheet of paper sitting in my typewriter. When Julia returned from work she sensed all was not well.

"What's wrong . . . what's happened?" she asked, obviously noticing something strange about me; or more strange than usual.

"Nothing . . . nothing's happened. Why do you ask?"

"I don't know . . . it's just you look odd . . . strange. Are you sure everything's alright?"

"Yes of course. It's been a difficult day, I've hit a block; it happens every so often. I'm sure tomorrow will be different."

"Come on Tom, I know you too well; something's happened hasn't it?"

"Well yes," I said, feeling annoyed at the transparency of my cover.

"Don't tell me, they don't want your book . . . that's it isn't it? . . . It's either that or something to do with that creepy Vince . . ."

"No, you are right . . . it's Stubbs. He called round here this morning. I heard a knock on the door just after you'd left . . . opened it and there he was standing outside. I . . ."

"Oh I don't believe it. What did he want? How did he know we were here?"

"There was an article in the paper about my book deal. He'd seen it, and said he wanted to congratulate me on my success. He. . ."

"He's after more money isn't he? Don't tell me I know that's why he came here. Oh my God you should never have given him that money in the first place. People like that think they're on to a good thing. Anyway what happened?"

"Well nothing really. He brought a bottle of champagne with him and suggested he and I had a drink to celebrate."

"Oh that's weird. That's really weird. And he didn't ask you for any more money?"

"No, nothing like that. I think he really is just lonely."

"How long did he stay for?"

"Not long . . . ten minutes or so. I told him I was busy and he left. He said things were going well his end, and that he was thinking of setting up again as a photographer, renting a studio; you know that sort of thing . . . and that was it."

I was acutely aware of the difference between being economical with the truth and lying. I was able to justify my ad lib embellishment about the photographic studio in my own mind; not only would it add a touch of credence to my lies, but my reasoning suggested that if I'd told her the truth, she would unintentionally put us both in *far more* danger by contacting the police. I hated myself for it. If I'd told her in the first place exactly how volatile and dangerous Stubbs was, it might have been a different matter. Now it was too late; there could be no going back. 'What a tangled web we weave when first we practice . . .' ran through my mind when I suddenly realised the champagne bottle had been hidden in the outhouse. 'Perhaps when she's changing upstairs I'll go and retrieve it and put it back in the rubbish bin', I pondered. It was vital now though for me to watch her every move from now until it's safely back in the bin. If she'd put something in the bin before going upstairs and hadn't noticed it before . . . it would be difficult to explain why it had suddenly appeared. How complicated life can become!

"I don't like this at all," she said. "There's something very disturbing about that sort of behaviour. Didn't you ask him how he found our new address?"

"No, to be honest I was completely taken aback at the image of him standing outside the door when I opened it . . . I forgot to mention, I mean . . ."

"Oh Tom you are an idiot. That's the first thing you should have thought of. Well the next time he chooses to call round here . . . and I bet there will be . . ."

"What do you mean?" I interrupted.

"He'll call again . . . there's no doubt about it . . . people like that . . .you've must tell him . . .you know . . .you can do it politely but firmly . . ."

"Yes, you're right I agree . . . Now how about a drink?" I said hoping to steer her away from the subject.

That evening Clive and Rachel had been invited to the house for a barbecue. Or to describe it more succinctly: an attempt at a barbecue. On the few previous occasions we'd tried this; something always went wrong. The first couple of times I failed to get the wretched coals to burn which resulted in Julia cooking food on the old kitchen range and then carrying it all out into the garden. The last time, everything miraculously went according to plan until my conspiracy theory intervened causing the skies to open up without warning soaking us all to the skin, whereupon the whole thing had to be abandoned.

Normally, I would have loved the idea but I knew only too well that the conversation for a major part of the evening would be centred on Stubbs and I was sick to death of worrying about what was going to happen next. None of them had any idea of the true dilemma facing me and the more they talked about it, the more detached and isolated I felt.

By somehow detaching myself from reality, I concentrated on finishing the book. By the end of July I had achieved this objective. A synopsis and the first three chapters had already received the approval of Jane Phillips; my agent, it was now just a matter of sending off the remainder of it and keeping my fingers crossed. Writing over the past few weeks had certainly preoccupied my thoughts. Now though that the book was finished, acute anxiety began to rear its ugly head once more. My tired brain was being continually bombarded with fears and nagging doubts about everything. I knew that time was running out and there was no plan to fall back on. If all went well, by the end of September the builder would be starting work on the house. I was banking on the hope that my book would not only meet with everyone's approval but that the money for it would be sitting in my bank account by then. These worries though paled into insignificance when I thought about the menacing figure of Stubbs.

Being idle, I quickly discovered was mentally destructive. I spent many days drafting letters to him explaining why his demands were unreasonable and how unfair it was of him to keep pestering us for money. Whilst writing these phlegmatic assessments of the morality of the situation (or lack of it), I convinced myself that by hitting the right formula and phrasing the letters in a certain style which highlighted irrefutably the inequitable nature of such demands, he would be compelled to reconsider the position. However as I never posted any of these, there was really little chance that however misguided; my objective would be achieved.

The endless days of waiting and inactivity resulted in the unwelcome nightly panic attacks returning. Julia was becoming increasingly alarmed when night after night I'd wake up gasping for breath. She would frequently find me pacing up and down the kitchen in the early hours looking as if my time had come. When things came to a head after nearly a week of this she insisted that I should go and see the doctor. After carrying out numerous tests and finding nothing physically wrong with me, the doctor diagnosed stress.

An appointment was booked for me to see a stress counsellor, and a further suggestion was made that I should embark upon some strenuous physical activity during the day to make me tired at night. I didn't like the sound of this at all. House maintenance, decorating and gardening were all very noble pursuits, but apart from the fact that I was unable to engender little enthusiasm for them; I considered my natural forte was writing. I was of the opinion that it would be far better to employ people who knew what they were doing rather the 'dabble' with things I was completely useless at or didn't understand. Julia though, tolerant as she was under the circumstances, was finding it increasingly difficult to accept this philosophy; particularly as we didn't have the money to pay anyone, and the house was falling apart around us.

During the second week of August, I finally received the news I'd been waiting for: the second book was accepted. According to Jane Phillips I would, with any luck, be receiving the money for this within the next two or three weeks. Although obviously overjoyed at this: the stress and tension increased for me knowing that Stubbs would soon return and demand the rest of *his* money.

It was around this time that a diversion of sorts occurred with the arrival of Julia's parents. Despite her well intentioned efforts at putting them off at least until we had the basic amenities; they were 'coming down south' anyway, as Steven; Julia's father had to attend a business meeting at the conference centre in Brighton. They'd met me once before when I was living with Julia prior to our break up. Julia's mother Rita tolerated me, but undoubtedly thought her daughter could have done a lot better. She at sixty, was still a good looking woman but like her daughter; manipulative, and not exactly easy. When she'd heard that Julia and I were back together her response was lukewarm at best. When Julia broke the news to her that I'd had thrown in my job and a promising career to write she was dismissive to put it mildly. 'Did' Julia know what she was doing living with an 'unemployed' writer? She was quite unable to accept that my employment *was that* of writing. The fact that I was self employed and stayed at home all day was all the proof she needed; although her attitude did change slightly when Julia told her about the book advances.

I found Steven much easier to get on with although he was undoubtedly quite boring and certainly henpecked. The ultra middle class lifestyle they led in a much closed community in Redruth in Cornwall was the acme of everything I was striving to avoid. The thought of their bridge evenings and select little 'drinks' gatherings where in my eyes they would gloat in their own self satisfaction; were completely abhorrent.

As they didn't know Brighton at all it was agreed that Julia and I would meet up with them for afternoon tea in the Grand Hotel where they were staying. As Steven's conference was on Monday they'd decided to travel down on the Saturday to make a long weekend of it. My hackles began to rise prematurely when I was instructed to shave off three days growth and wear a collar and tie for the occasion.

The irritation I felt at having to wear a tight collar and tie on a hot summer's day was nothing compared with the frustration caused by the lack of parking spaces. After driving slowly around in the congested holiday traffic I was forced to drop Julia off outside and drive nearly into Hove before I found a space. When I walked into the hotel I was hot and bothered and in a foul frame of mind. After the usual forced pleasantries we all advanced towards the restaurant as if 'tea' simply couldn't wait a moment longer.

"Oh I'm so happy for you," Rita said to me, "it must be a wonderful feeling having a book published . . . well two!"

"Yes it is good news," I agreed.

"And of course it's such good news about The Rectory. Julia sent us some photos of the outside and it really does look impressive."

"Yes, it is. But mummy, I'm warning you, there's an awful lot of work to do on it though, we're living like Hill Billy's at the moment," Julia said. "It's not quite so bad now that the weather's warmer, but when we first moved in it was difficult."

"Well, now that things are looking up . . . I mean as far as your books are concerned you'll soon be able to get people in to sort it all out for you," Steven added.
I tried to respond to this, but didn't get a chance.

"Oh well, perhaps after tea you'll show us over it," Rita said.

"Yes, if you don't mind squeezing into my old wreck we'll go back as soon as we've had tea. Tom will go and get the car and he can drop you back here again afterwards," Julia said trying to avoid my piercing gaze.

After devouring three buttered scones, numerous little triangular sandwiches, a couple of chocolate cakes and three cups of Lapsang Souchong tea; I felt slightly sick. I felt even sicker when I saw the bill which Steven thankfully scooped off the table before I could make the requisite polite noises which such occasions demand.

Forty minutes later Julia's battered old Fiesta drew up outside The Rectory. At the sight of it, or more precisely; the garden; Julia's father who seemed to be moribund in the car on the way there, suddenly came to life again. As if part of some rehearsed programme, he walked determinedly around the garden reeling off the names of various plants and shrubs that would be ideally suited to this position or that position . . . how well they would grow and so on. I still feeling queasy; I peered at him with a vapid expressionless face hoping he wasn't expecting a positive response. Julia and her mother were preoccupied picking blackberry's that were according to Rita, the juiciest ones she'd ever tasted.

As they stepped inside the gloomy kitchen from the dazzling August sunlight it took a few moments for their eyes to adjust. A look of disbelief came over Rita's face. The hitherto fixed pleasant smile was instantly transformed into one of shock and horror. What was this 'unemployed' writer doing to her precious daughter? Was the man totally mad? Her face said it all.

"Oh . . . *I see what you mean*," she said, "You've certainly got your work cut out here."

"Yes I know, but it's full of character," Julia said enthusiastically, "come and see the rest of it."

"Nice and spacious," was all Steven could find to say about it; obviously far more interested in the garden.

"But this is going to cost you a fortune to put right isn't it?" Rita stated as she and Julia walked into the front reception room.

"No, not really," Julia responded with an air of nonchalance. "We've got a builder who's going to do all the major stuff and he'll be starting soon; then Tom and I will do all the decorating."

"Oh," said Rita whispering, "I didn't realize Tom was good at that sort of thing."

"Oh yes, he loves it," she said, mistakenly imagining that I was well out of earshot.

I was in fact just outside giving Steven a guided tour of the various outhouses, one of which I was told should be used as a potting shed. I couldn't help but agree with this suggestion despite not knowing what went on in such a building. Once the initial shock had worn off, both of Julia's parents were in no doubt as to the potential of the property but both of them failed to understand why we needed such a big house.

My attempt at feigning a hospitable front by requesting they stay for more tea was flatly refused after a Rita had carried out a surreptitious examination of the kitchen. It seemed they were both now anxious to retreat to the comparative safety of The Grand Hotel.

Revelling in the joy of having got away lightly was premature. Just as they were getting out of the car outside the hotel, Steven said, "See you both for lunch tomorrow then."

"What?" I asked looking at him aghast.

"Oh perhaps Julia didn't mention . . . we thought it would be nice if we all had lunch together tomorrow . . . here . . . at the hotel. The food is evidently very good, top class chefs and all that."

"Right . . . that's terrific. I'll look forward to it," I said trying to sound excited at this pleasant surprise. This really was the last straw. I'd put myself out in the most self sacrificing way imaginable to appear sociable and polite and now . . . It was Sunday lunch. Not *just* Sunday lunch, but Sunday lunch in a loathsome pretentious hotel on a hot summer's day. What could possibly be more unpleasant than that!

'Oh well thank God they *did* live in Cornwall or things could be a lot worse', I told myself as I sat in a traffic jam watching with disdain the thousands of morbidly obese tourists and day trippers milling around the Palace Pier.

What might normally have been a thirty minute round trip took me an hour and a half. When I did arrive back at the house I was scarlet faced, soaked in perspiration and thoroughly disgruntled. To make matters worse; before we'd left, I'd completely forgotten to top up the coals in the primitive kitchen range which meant we had nothing to cook on and no hot water. The pleasures of the simple life and 'making do' were evaporating fast.

"Mummy thinks you're ever so clever," Julia announced on my return, "and they love the house."

"Good *I am* pleased," I said sarcastically.

"They were saying that it's such a pity they live so far away; Daddy would have liked to have helped you with the garden."

"Yes such a shame," I agreed with a notable lack of sincerity in my voice as I burrowed further inside the old range trying to extract the ashes. "It would have been such bliss, just the two of us doing some serious bonding; discussing the merits of suitable planting areas and soil composition for our rhododendrons."

"Oh don't be silly, you know what I mean."

"Unfortunately I do."

The Grand Hotel was bustling with life when we arrived. In order to minimize the frustration of trying to park on Brighton sea front we'd walked there. I was even more irritable and downcast than the day before. The weather was hot; one of the rare days in England when the temperatures hit the early thirties. With not only a collar and tie, but a heavy Harris Tweed jacket as well; I was cursing and blaspheming continuously until we arrived. Trying to be sociable for two whole days was an enormous challenge which now I was finding it almost impossible to cope with.

My vituperative condemnation of the guests hovering around the cocktail bar for pre dinner drinks was openly expressed on my red sweaty face which I have no doubt was grimacing as if in agony. When we were eventually escorted to our table by a particularly unctuous restaurant manager, I felt as if I might spontaneously combust.

Throughout the meal, try as they did, they couldn't extract more than a few words from me. Several times Julia asked me if I was alright and what was I thinking about? The last time she enquired I was strongly tempted to tell her the truth: that sitting in this loathsome hotel restaurant being surrounded by a lot of pseudo middle class pretentious bores was akin to torture.

After what seemed an eternity, the lunch came to an end. Steven again picked up the bill leaving a tip that I estimated would have kept me in Shepherds pie for a month at Albion Mansions. I then unexpectedly made a great effort to tell them how much I'd enjoyed it and how nice it was to see them both again. This of course made them not just uneasy but a little wary sensing nothing could have been further from the truth.

They'd never met a writer before perhaps they were *all* a bit strange and detached at times.

My joy at imagining this unpleasant encounter had now reached its natural conclusion was short lived. Just when I was expecting to bid them farewell and insist they enjoyed the rest of their stay, Rita suggested that a constitutional along the seafront might benefit them after the heavy meal. After two pints of beer, for glasses of red wine and a brandy, I now had a thumping headache. The prospect of a three mile walk along the bustling promenade in the blazing sun didn't hold much appeal. The agonised grimacing reappeared involuntarily on my face as the four of us headed off towards the pier.

Dodging between the swarms of people shouting and screaming, hauling crimson faced tetchy overtired children behind them was a serious test of endurance. To further exacerbate the situation Julia declared that her parents couldn't possibly go back without having been on the pier. The pier on a day like this, as far as I was concerned, equated with Dante's Inferno. Scowling bitterly, I gave Julia a long disapproving stare, suspecting that this was her way of paying me back for my subdued manner over lunch. She knew exactly how much I hated this sort of claustrophobic human congestion. As we stood by the entrance I was seriously considering feigning a heart attack or perhaps a fit . . . anything to avoid prolonging this torture.

A welcome breeze coming off the sea helped to cool me down and gradually the aggressive thumping inside my head decreased to the tempo of a normal headache. Having fought our way from one end of the pier to the other and back again, things were now drawing to a close. Having said their goodbyes, Julia's parents weaved their way back to the hotel, whilst Julia and I walked off in the other direction back to The Rectory.

Delighted that this ordeal was over, I spent most of the next morning making notes for a new book I had in mind. The basic plot was not too dissimilar to the other two, except this one featured a female killer. At lunch time I paused for a break, made some tea, and was just about to take it out to an old deck chair in the garden when I noticed the post had been delivered. Sifting through it I found a letter from Jane Phillips; inside, was another cheque for twenty thousand, five hundred and ninety three pounds and seventy five pence. Discarding the tea and a sandwich I'd made, I marched off to the bank to pay it in.

My initial euphoria wore off quickly knowing that in a week's time Stubbs would be returning to divest me of the bulk of the money . . . Money which was to be paid to the builder. My mood deteriorated rapidly as I considered the injustice that was taking place. Something would have to be done; I knew 'the conspiracy' as I called it was evil, but this would drive anyone to madness. I estimated that after tax and national insurance; I would be left with about seventeen thousand. If I were to give Stubbs the thirteen thousand he was demanding, that would leave me with around four thousand pounds. No this is totally ridiculous, I told myself. I was now reaching a critical stage in my life. If I so much as mentioned, even jokingly, that I was thinking of giving him the money we were going to give the builder, Julia would leave me immediately; and who could blame her? No, the fact of the matter was that Stubbs could do what he liked but he wasn't getting another penny off us.

When Julia returned from work she was of course delighted that the cheque had come through as anticipated. The builder was due to start in four week's time . . . but perhaps he might be able to start sooner now that we had the money. I was instructed to phone him and find out if this was possible. It turned out that we were in luck; as the weather had been good for the past few weeks he'd been able to 'steam on' as he put it and could bring their job forward by two or three week's. He'd be able to give us a definite starting date by the end of the week. In the mean time he was going to arrange for the scaffolding to be erected, and would be dropping some plant and equipment round to the site in the next few days.

Julia couldn't contain her excitement at the prospect of escaping from the Stone Age as she put it. We'd lived 'like gypsies' for the past five months, and yes it might be character building, but she was now sick to death of it. I would have loved to have shared her joy but was unable to . . . The clock was ticking . . . the noose was getting tighter; my chest pains returned . . . I wasn't looking very well at all. The nights for me were the worst time; I dreaded going to bed knowing that within ten minutes Julia would be sound asleep, while I would lie next to her sweating, with my heart pounding like a drum and then the gasping and fighting for breath would start. For the past couple of week's I'd barely slept at all. My worst fear was the nightmares. They were becoming more terrifying and gruesome as the days progressed. The one that recurred most, was a very vivid one of me being tortured; being held down, while all sorts of unspeakable atrocities were inflicted. The pain that seemed real, reached excruciating levels resulting in me waking up screaming in terror. But the dream I feared most of all was of killing someone myself. When this occurred, I would wake up in a state of absolute trauma, it took me several minutes to fully comprehend that it hadn't really happened. 'It was just a dream', I'd keep saying to myself but still found it hard to believe, and invariably I wouldn't be able to get back to sleep again.

A series of counselling appointments had now been arranged by my doctor. Having attended the first of these, I had little faith in the supposed benefits. The once weekly meetings were being held in a room at the rear of the surgery, and were conducted by a recently qualified 'stress therapist'. I considered her to be in her early twenties with no experience of life whatsoever. For the whole fifty minutes she would encourage me to talk about my life and see if I could identify the areas that were causing me stress. I speculated with perverse amusement on how she might have reacted had I told her the truth. The problem here was that Julia had become increasingly concerned about my state of mind, and as the doctor had suggested it, I was really obliged to attend.

Probably as a manifestation of boredom; I decided to tell her about my nightmares. I could tell immediately that this had not just unnerved her; she appeared to nodding politely to me whilst feeling around for the alarm button as I went into graphic detail. As I walked home afterwards, I was regretting this foolishness. More likely than not, I would receive a referral to see a psychiatrist. Or perhaps I might even be sectioned *in absentia* before I could attend another session.

Three days later I went along to the bank carrying a smart leather attaché case that had last seen service when I was with the insurance company. Presenting the cashier with a cheque made out to cash for thirteen thousand pounds was uncannily reminiscent of the previous large withdrawal. The cashier looked at me suspiciously, whispered something I couldn't hear and disappeared. A few minutes' later eyes were upon me from every corner of the bank. Then predictably, the servile manager glided across to me from somewhere and declared what a great pleasure it was to see me again. I pre-empted what I knew was about to take place again.

"Yes I know it's a large sum of money. I don't require investment advice thank you. I would be grateful if you would just get the money for me in used tens and twenties."

"Of course sir," he replied, "if you'd be kind enough to follow me; we won't keep you too long. I'll arrange for our cashier to get this for you."

After a further five minutes of grovelling and patronising small talk in the manager's office, a bony consumptive looking clerk knocked on the door and brought in several cloth bags and placed them on the manager's desk.

"Now let's check this to make sure it's all there. You don't want to leave here and find we've short changed you now, ha, ha."

I stared at the pile of notes for a few seconds mesmerized by the bulk of it. Trying to act as if it were an every day occurrence, I stacked the piles of notes evenly into the attaché case whilst endeavouring to avoid eye contact or for that matter, any further questions.

The bank manager was undoubtedly beside himself with curiosity. He deviously tried again to glean even a clue as to what I was up to. He certainly wasn't going to find out. The thought of *him* lying awake wondering what this money could be for gave me immense pleasure.

On arriving back at The Rectory, I unlocked the garage placed the attaché case on an upturned tea chest, opened it to reveal the neatly stacked piles of cash and covered it with an old sack. I then pulled the old wooden doors shut and re-fixed the padlock, giving it a good tug to make sure it was secure. A few minutes later I was seated in front of my typewriter continuing with the second chapter of my new book. At least today one thing has been accomplished successfully, I muttered to myself.

Chapter 10

Early the next morning, Martin Davis the builder arrived to run through everything with us again prior to starting. All being well, he and his men would be here in a week's time. He suggested that in the mean time I might knock down one of the derelict garden sheds and pile the old bricks up outside the kitchen as some of this would be required for hardcore for the new kitchen floor. I asked him if he minded us staying in the house whilst the work was going on. Although he seemed quite incredulous at this, he didn't seem to mind. As long as we kept out of his way it was up to us, was his less than diplomatic response.

Oh there was one thing though . . . he'd had to pay out a lot of cash recently and was running short of it. If there was any possibility of him being paid in *'ready's'* he would appreciate it and he might even be able to let us have a small discount!

As soon as Julia had left for work I settled in front of my typewriter determined to press on with the new book. Tomorrow was Saturday; this was my last chance to produce something before the weekend. Anything else could wait until then; the times when I could write seemed to have become scarcer and had to be seized upon.

Martin reckoned the whole job would take about four weeks from start to finish. I already foresaw that little writing would be achieved during that time with all the noise and general disruption. Rather than following a consistent flow; my writing was produced in fits and starts depending upon my mood. Sometimes I'd sit for hours in front of a blank sheet of paper with my mind in a vacuum; then suddenly I'd be charged with inspiration; tap away frantically for a few hours before reverting to the former state. Much of course depended on my previous night's sleep; or lack of it. People's perception of how it was actually done, or how writers worked, bore no resemblance to the reality of it. Even I imagined before taking it up seriously that a sort of mechanical procedure took place. You sat in front of a typewriter every day for so many hours and produced a certain number of words. Oh if only this were true!

Obviously Julia had a destructive tendency I'd not yet witnessed. On Saturday when I started demolishing the remains of the old garden shed; she was desperate to have a go. Smacking the crumbling brickwork with a fourteen pound sledge hammer produced screams of ecstasy from her. I was convinced that I'd got the short straw though having to carry bucket loads of bricks thirty yards up to the house in the burning August heat.

By lunchtime the job was done. I sat in the old deckchair conducting a full examination of my blistered fingers while Julia busied herself in the kitchen making sandwiches for our well deserved lunch.

Reluctantly I had to admit that I wasn't *exactly* cut out for building work. If anything I felt slightly cheated that I'd been coerced into this and was beginning to question quite how it had happened. After all we'd agreed a price for the work that was to be done: this was taking liberties. Perhaps it should be viewed as an omen of what awaited me. Yes, I'd have to treat any further casual requests from Martin with a degree of circumspection otherwise I could be put to use as an unpaid skivvy when the work commenced.

A few days later I was positioned in my deck chair contemplating initially the plot of my book, but as seemed to be happening more and more these days; my mind was beginning to wander. Distracted at first by a couple of giant bumble bees that were frantically chasing each other; my attention was then abruptly focused upon a brightly coloured butterfly that was fluttering around my feet. Magpies, finches and crows were landing on the overgrown apple tree a few yards away; singing a few discordant notes and taking off again. Every so often a gigantic seagull would swoop down, land precariously on the pile of bricks outside the kitchen, and watch me with interest. A blissful serenity ensued.

The sound of footsteps walking up the unmade road caused me to look up again with a start. Squinting from the sun, I could just make out the figure of Stubbs. As he drew closer my heart dropped. The now familiar icy chill ran down my spine. This is it, I said to myself . . . it's now or never . . . stay calm that's the important thing.

"Working hard I see," Stubbs said sarcastically as he approached.

"Yes, I am actually."

"Well I thought I'd better drop by and see how things were going."

"Yes of course. It's the money you've come for I presume?"

"Well what do you think?"

"Hmm, to be honest I hadn't imagined there might be any other reason. As it happens though, you're in luck. The cheque came through last week and as soon as it cleared I withdrew the amount you wanted."

"Now, what a sensible fellow you are. Well I certainly don't want to hold you up, I can see you're very busy; so if we. . ."

"Yes of course," I said keeping both eyes firmly fixed upon him. "If you follow me we'll go and get it."
I got up slowly, put my notes on the deckchair and placed a stone on top of them.

"Just to stop the wind blowing them away," I explained.
Stubbs just looked at me curiously with a frozen grimace, and followed me over to the garage.

"It's in here," I said, "I'll just go and get the key, I won't be a minute."
Stubbs said nothing; just stood there with the same fixed contemptuous expression. Twenty seconds later I returned with the key; unlocked the padlock and pulled one of the old wooden doors ajar; the bottom of it making an unpleasant grating noise on the concrete. Stubbs then slowly followed me in to the semi darkness of the garage.

"It's over there," I said pointing to the back of the garage, "under that sack."

"Right," said Stubbs walking over to the spot I'd pointed to. He bent down and pulled the sack away revealing the open attaché case full of money.

"Nice to see you've kept to your wor . . . Aaagh! . . . You fucking . . . Aaagh!"

Stubbs slumped over the attaché case; his eyes rolled back and his body seemed to be violently twitching. I stood over him transfixed with the crowbar held tightly in my hand. After a few seconds his eyes closed and he was perfectly still. I couldn't work out whether he was still alive. There was no blood. I bent down and placed a hand on his face. It was still warm. Terrified that he might suddenly come round; I lifted the crowbar above my head and hit him again with all my might across the back of the head. All that could be heard was a dull thud. I saw a trickle of bright red blood oozing from his head. 'Yes he must be dead', I reassured myself. After careful inspection of the crowbar was carried out to ensure no part of him had stuck to it, I hung it back on a rusty nail spiked into the brickwork.

I grabbed his arms by the wrists and dragged him out of the corner alongside the pit. The next job I wasn't looking forward to. Slowly and methodically I dug around in his pockets. Having satisfied myself that everything had been removed I sifted through an assortment of keys, small change, a cigarette lighter and a large wallet from the back pocket. I removed a packet of cigarettes from the top pocket of his shirt and lighted one. 'Pity you're not able to share a last cigarette with me', I said kneeling besides him, and then convulsed with insane terrified laughter. I'd obviously struck lucky, I thought, when turning out the contents of his wallet revealed a thick wad of fifty pound notes. 'Must keep a check on things', I told myself as I counted out twenty fifty pound notes, four twenties, two tens, and a fiver. I placed the driving license and other bits and pieces back inside the wallet and threw them into the inspection pit. I stuffed the money and keys into my pocket. I grabbed hold of his leather belt with one hand and an arm with the other and dragged the limp body across the floor until it was directly over the pit. One hefty push and . . . thud! Thankfully he'd landed face down. His left arm had got snagged on the side of the pit and was unnaturally bent up behind him. I rejoiced; I'd never have to see that frightening angry face again. I checked around and was relieved to discover that the blood gently oozing from his head had congealed in his hair and not marked the garage floor. After all I'd got enough to do right now without him creating further work for me.

I was dreading the next job. 'More labouring' I said to myself. 'It's a good job I've had some practice'.

Two hours later he was covered in a couple of feet of hardcore. 'Time to stop for lunch.' I said to myself. The immediate problem facing me now was that the inspection pit was still only half full. I urgently needed more hardcore but couldn't take anymore from outside the kitchen as it would be needed for the new kitchen floor.

'Certainly gives you an appetite, this sort of work', I said to myself as I sat in my deck chair munching away on a pork pie. Suddenly I was filled with inspiration. The concrete base of the shed we'd demolished still had to be broken up and removed. This would surely provide enough material to fill the pit up to within six inches or so of the garage floor level. Yes it might be hard work, but this would do the job admirably. Once that was done all I had to do was ask Martin to concrete over the top of it. There would probably be some concrete left over from the kitchen floor anyway.

With renewed vigour I started hitting it with the fourteen pound sledge hammer. With sweat running down my face stinging my eyes, I continued relentlessly. Within less than half an hour the whole floor looked like a gigantic broken biscuit. All I had to do now was pick out the broken lumps of concrete and carry them down to the garage. Much harder work than I'd realised! By five o'clock the job was done. Julia will be impressed, I told myself as I surveyed my handiwork. Just a matter now of hiding the case of money and the worst part of the job was over.

Life was now worth living again; everything looked rosy . . . except . . . except for one thing . . .

I had recovered some of the money I'd given Stubbs: but what about the rest of it? It was possible that the remainder of the cash; nearly eleven thousand pounds, was stashed away in his room at Albion Mansions. The chances of it still being there were reasonably high. There was also the letter: the letter from the insurance company, with my name at the bottom of it. This had to be retrieved at all cost. The police weren't stupid; they wouldn't view this as coincidence. The photographs as well: better if they were not lying around giving them something to poke their noses in.   I had been thinking about this for a long time. I now had the keys and a small window of opportunity before Mrs Hoskins started to wonder where he was. Once she had contacted the police to report him missing; they would surely carry out a search of his belongings in the hope of finding a clue to his whereabouts and it would then be too late. The money was mine and I was entitled to it. Had he not had been so greedy; he would have been alive to spend it. Hopefully he hadn't already done so. No . . . justice had to be done! He certainly wouldn't be missed for at least a couple of days.

Julia, when she returned from work, was highly impressed with my industrious activities, although a little perplexed as to why I'd wanted to fill the inspection pit in.

"What was it for anyway?" she enquired, standing over it.

"Well . . . for inspections I suppose."

"Golly; when you think about it, it would have been the ideal place to bury a body," she said emitting a husky guffaw of laughter.

"Yes that's true; it's certainly the sort of thing you read about, perhaps I'll bear that in mind for my next book."

Despite the day of back breaking toil; I was in remarkably good spirits feeling as if a great weight had been lifted from me. Things were now fitting into place. Martin would be starting the following week and now we had the money to pay him. Yes, everything so far was going according to plan. Tonight, or to be more precise at three o'clock in the morning, I'd let myself into Albion Mansions. Without doubt everyone at this time would be fast asleep. I'd tiptoe up to Stubbs's room, find the money and the envelope containing my letter and the photos and creep out again. The trickiest part would getting up and leaving the house without waking Julia. Having thought this out I'd invested in two bottles of

212

wine knowing that after four or five glasses Julia would sleep through an earthquake.

In order for the plan to proceed it was essential that I stayed awake. This was without doubt the most difficult part. Just after midnight we climbed into bed and within five minutes Julia was sound asleep. When my head touched the pillow and I stretched my weary and aching limbs that desperately needed to relax after the day's toil, I had serious doubts about my resolve to continue. At two fifteen I must get up as quietly as a mouse; carry my clothes downstairs; get dressed and go. I couldn't very well set the alarm clock. The walk to Albion Mansions would take half an hour at the most. A few minutes inside the building and half an hour back. If all went well I'd be gone for just over an hour. I could stash the money away (assuming it was there) in the outhouse where I'd left the door unlocked, and creep back into bed. In the morning we could be better of to the tune of twelve thousand pounds, and it was my money after all.

As the seconds ticked by I was trying to keep my nerve and more importantly; trying to keep awake. I tried to think about other things, but to no avail. What if somebody was still up once I was inside and saw me? Very unlikely, but perhaps I should think of a reason why I would be there at that time, and how did I get in? 'No, better not to think about it', I told myself. Having lived there for six months I knew the whole house would be as quiet as the grave at this time.

By one o'clock I was fighting to stay awake. My back ached; my legs were throbbing and my stinging eyes were begging my eyelids to drop. Julia snorted, let out a groan and turned over. The tension was too much; as soon as she'd settled again I decided that was it . . . enough; It was now one fifteen . . . an hour to go. Better to get up *now* I told myself. It would be impossible to lie there any longer trying to stay awake. In slow motion I slid out of bed, picked up my clothes and crept downstairs.

A mug of strong coffee and a couple of cigarettes seemed to settle my nerves a little. At two fifteen, fifteen minutes earlier than planned I drew back the bolts on the front door and started my mission. Extreme care was needed not to make a noise walking on the unmade track leading away from the house. The weather was perfect for a nocturnal stroll: magically quiet and still with a full moon providing all the illumination I needed to get onto the main road. Walking at a leisurely pace I arrived at Albion Mansions at ten to three. Pausing outside the Crown and Anchor, I lighted a cigarette and carried out a careful surveillance of the façade of Albion Mansions. Just as expected . . . no lights on anywhere. A few windows were open which was understandable; it was an unusually warm night.

Taking a deep breath, I crossed the road, tiptoed up to the front door and inserted the mortise key turning it slowly to avoid any metallic clicks. It was just a case now of inserting the cylinder key and gently pushing the door open. 'Must remember the wretched bell', I said to myself. By pushing the door extremely slowly, a couple of inches at a time it was possible to get in, or out, without the shrill clanging noise this always made. Once inside, the door was pushed to employing the same methodology with the exception now that my hands were shaking. Mrs Hoskins; I knew, was a light sleeper; any slight mishaps at ground floor level would be right outside her room. She'd be sure to come bumbling out at the slightest noise. Treading on the inside corners of the stairs to avoid them creaking; I started my ascent with a penlight torch in one hand and the keys in the other. I was just approaching the fourth floor when I heard a noise: a door being opened. I crouched down on the staircase trying to make myself as small as possible and listened. Yes, somebody had come out of a room on the fourth floor and walked across to the bathroom. I thought it must be Benson releasing some of the Crown and Anchors 'best'. Hearing the cistern flush and some raucous coughing confirmed my suspicions were right. A couple of minutes later Benson was back in his room and the climb continued.

On the fifth floor I felt more at ease knowing that Stubbs's room was unoccupied and it was possible that my old room was still vacant. A strange eerie feeling came over me as I entered the room of my victim. I was gripped with fear still believing that he would suddenly appear from somewhere. Gently I closed the door and switched on the light. Everything was much as I'd remembered it. A new bottle of whisky stood on the little coffee table with a large overflowing ash tray next to it.

After a quick rummage through a chest of drawers and the bedside cabinet, I started on the wardrobe. Stuffed behind piles of shoes at the bottom I found what I was looking for. I recognised the plastic bag. In a burst of excitement I pulled it out causing an incredible din as a pile of shoes that had been stacked on top of each other fell out onto the floor.

I certainly wasn't going to count it but it seemed roughly about the same size and weight that I remembered. More carefully now, I stacked the shoes up again and closed the wardrobe door. 'Right, so far so good', I muttered to myself and stood for a moment by the door trying to regain my composure. 'Oh shit', I muttered, 'where can he have put *that* envelope'? I opened the wardrobe door again and felt around the top shelf: No; only clothes. Where could it be? I knelt down and looked under the bed. Ah! There was an old suitcase. 'Must be in there', I said to myself. I dragged it out and heaved a sigh of relief finding that it wasn't locked. The case was stuffed full of papers and photos. I was in luck; the brown envelope on top was it. I folded it over twice and pushed it into my back pocket: closed the case and pushed it back under the bed. Once outside of the room I was suddenly overcome with a bone chilling fear and started to panic. I knew at a push, by making a run for it, I could be back out on the street in less than thirty seconds and that's where I desperately wanted to be. Biting my lip and with my face contorted with stress and fear I started tiptoeing down the stairs. Getting myself down to the ground floor seemed to take an eternity. This was something I would never ever forget.

Now standing behind the main front door all I had to do was release the cylinder lock and open it slowly, but I was momentarily paralyzed with terror. My heart pounding like a pneumatic gun; swathed in perspiration, I stood there unable to move. I'd managed everything exceptionally well until now; what was happening to me? I wondered. Finally after a couple of minutes of taking deep breaths; my trembling hand released the latch and inch by inch and I pulled the door open. This was it; I was outside with the money. The last little job now was just to pull the door to and lock it. By inserting the key first I was able to hold the spring loaded latch back until the door was tight against the frame and then release it gently. Yes this went perfectly. I then hesitated for a moment. Should I lock it with the mortise key? 'Yes', I decided, that's how it was; 'better not leave any clues', I thought, and very carefully inserted the key and turned it twice before creeping down the steps onto the pavement.

Back at The Rectory I carefully pulled the outhouse door open and went inside to count the money which was still bundled up in polythene packets. Exactly nine thousand pounds was there. This together with the money I'd taken from the dead mans wallet meant I'd recovered exactly ten thousand, one hundred and five pounds of the money I'd given him. Not only that, but I would never have to see his menacing loathsome face again. After stuffing the cash into an empty weed killer tin, I closed the door and went into the house. The envelope containing my letter and the photos went straight into the fire of the kitchen range.

Julia was still fast asleep. I would have loved to have woken her to tell her we were now ten thousand pounds richer, but exactly how this came about would have to remain my secret and only mine for the rest of my life. I hadn't yet thought of how I would explain this sudden windfall, but there was plenty of time to think about that. Gently I pulled the duvet back and slid into bed. Within three minutes I was sleeping like a baby with a broad satisfied grin on my face.

"Couldn't you sleep last night?" Julia asked me in the morning.

"No, I woke up after another extraordinary dream," I replied.

"What happened? . . . In your dream, what happened?"

"Well, I can't remember it all, but part of it was terrifying. I seem to remember the end of it was better, at least I came out of it one piece."

"I think part of the problem must be your fertile imagination. But if you're going to continue writing the sort of stuff you do then I suppose you ought to be grateful for that. When's your next appointment with the stress therapist?"

"On Thursday supposedly; although I suspect she's a bit out of her depth."

"Why do you say that?"

"Oh it's just . . .the last time I told her about a dream I'd had and I could see the fear and panic on her face. I expect she's having counselling herself now to try and get over it."

The following week the builder started stripping the roof, ripping out the kitchen range and all the old iron pipe work. My initial insouciance about making do was seriously challenged after the first week when we were reduced to squatting in one room upstairs with a camping gas stove to cook on and the only source of water being a temporary stand pipe outside the kitchen. Another little joy for us was the chemical toilet that Martin had lent us. This was sited in the outhouse.

Every time Julia had to use it, I would have to accompany her and wait outside the door in case a spider appeared.

By the end of the fourth week things were taking shape. The roof was finished: the kitchen had a new concrete floor and the pit in the garage had been concreted over. Most of the plumbing and central heating had been installed including a new bathroom and kitchen. There were of course numerous jobs that still needed doing but I was aware that Martin had just about completed the work he'd quoted for. Somehow or other I would have to come up with an explanation of we'd suddenly become ten thousand pounds better off. Once this was sorted out; Martin could be instructed to complete the rest of the work after which I could continue writing in peace. I loved the house; ever more so now that we had the basic amenities. One thing I hated though was any form of DIY; mainly because I wasn't in the least bit practical and usually made a complete mess of anything I ever attempted.

One task I really couldn't get out of was clearing the roof space of all the junk and debris that had accumulated over more than a century. Martin explained that if I did this whilst he was still there, he'd remove the rubbish in his truck and would also lay the insulation for me. This was the opportunity I had been waiting for. In the roof space there were a couple of old trunks. One of them was empty and the other was full of old documents. When Martin left that day; I retrieved the money I'd taken from Stubbs, took it out of the polythene packets, wrapped it up in an old curtain and placed it at the bottom of the trunk. What a lucky find this would be!

When Julia drove up in her old Fiesta; I ran out to greet her smiling all over my face.

"You'll never believe what I've found," I said.

"What do you mean," she said, completely mystified by my exuberance.

"Quick; come with me."

"It's nothing nasty is it?"

"I wouldn't exactly say that," I said as she followed me up the rickety ladder into the roof.

I opened the trunk, frantically throwing all the old papers out and pulled out the dirty old curtain.

"Open it up," I shouted.

"No . . . look; stop it Tom; I don't like this. What's inside it?"

"I think *you will* like it," I said grinning from ear to ear, as I undid the bundle revealing a large pile of fifty pound notes.

"Oh my God," she screamed, how much is there? Whose is it? How did it get there?"

"No idea. That's not our problem. It looks like a lot of money to me; let's count it," I said watching her shocked face.

"Ten thousand, exactly ten thousand pounds," I said laughing insanely.

"Oh, I can't believe it," she said, "do you think whoever left it there will remember and come back for it?"

"Not a chance."

"How can you be sure?"

"Because they're dead . . . if you remember, this was an executor's sale. That's probably a good enough reason."

Now at last I could proceed with the final part of my plan. Heaving a sigh of relief at not having to spend days carting all the debris down from the roof: Martin was instructed to do the job and to finish all the other outstanding items that I was dreading. We even had enough money to replace Julia's battered old Fiesta and even go off for a short holiday.

One afternoon a few weeks later, I was typing away; now more than half way through my new book when a loud urgent knocking at the front door made me jump out of my chair. When I opened it, two smartly dressed men introduced themselves.

"Sorry to disturb you. Tom Dunford is it?"

"Yes?"

"I'm D.C. Webb, and this is D.S Bradshaw. We're from Brighton C.I.D. We're just making some enquiries regarding a missing person and wondered if you would be kind enough to answer a few questions?"

I must have turned as white as a ghost. I hadn't expected this.

"Yes of course. What person are you talking about?"

"Well perhaps we might come in for a moment sir then we can explain."

"Yes . . . I'm sorry . . . I was in the middle of something; yes please come in."

"Right sir, we believe you may have known a Vincent Edward Stubbs, when you were living at 49 Albion Mansions is that correct?"

"Yes . . . well I mean I knew him vaguely. Why has he gone missing?"

"When was the last time you saw him?"

"I . . . I can't exactly remember. It's over six months ago certainly."

"Are you aware of any friends or relatives of his that might know of his whereabouts'?"

"No I'm afraid not. I only spoke to him a couple of times; his room was next to mine. Thinking about it, I did see him once in the pub; the Crown and Anchor one evening. I was there with some friends and he offered to buy us a drink: we thanked him but refused as we were going off to a restaurant. What's actually happened, can I ask?"

"Well sir, at the beginning of September the landlady and owner of the premises: Mrs Hoskins was concerned that he'd not shown up for meals that he'd agreed to take at the premises. After seven days with no word from him, she became increasing alarmed and contacted the police. Obviously she was worried something might have happened to him. Our officers entered his room with the landlady and could find no evidence to suggest he'd left . . . you know . . . moved . . . gone off somewhere. His car was also parked outside, so we have to treat it as a missing person case."

"Yes I understand. As I say, I haven't seen him since I was last living there. I do hope he's alright, he seemed like a very nice person to me. I think Mrs Hoskins mentioned that he'd recently lost his wife."

"Yes we believe that is correct sir. Well . . . thank you for your assistance. I assume it's unlikely, but if you do happen to see him we would be most grateful if you would contact Brighton police."

"Indeed of course, but I do think that's extremely unlikely; he'd have no reason to contact me, as I say I hardly knew the chap."

"No I understand, and thank you again for your time sir."

"Phew, thank goodness Julia wasn't here," I mumbled, as I closed the door behind them.

Now another slight dilemma presents itself. Do I tell her about this visit and the missing Stubbs or not? After pondering this for the rest of the day I decided I would have to. If they returned she would understandably be suspicious as to why I'd kept their visit a secret.

Later that evening I casually broached the subject as if it was of little significance.

"Oh I meant to tell you," I started, "we had a visit from the men in blue today."

"Men in blue? Who are you talking about?"

"The *old bill*, the police."

"Really, what did they want? Oh no don't tell me, they're after that money you found in the roof."

"No, no it's nothing to do with that. It's my old friend Stubbs. Evidently he's gone missing."

"Missing, what's that got to do with us? What do they mean missing . . . has something happened to him then?"

"Well, they don't know. They were saying that Mrs Hoskins my old landlady realized he wasn't turning up for meals and as he hadn't said anything to her about going away, she got worried, as she does and called the police."

"But why would they come round here . . . the police? I mean. Did you tell them that you'd given him the money?"

"No, I didn't mention it. There's not much point really. That's got nothing to do with him going missing. Unless . . .unless of course . . .ah yes I didn't think about that . . .he's probably flown off to South America with some young model and is now living it up on my money!"

"Oh well good riddance is all I can say if that's the case. Did you tell them that he'd been hanging around outside my flat before we moved? And did you tell them about . . ."

"No I didn't mention any of that. I just told them that I hadn't really had much contact with him. I said that if I saw him around I'd let them know."

"Well I hope we don't see him around."

"Yes, *so do I,*" I said, staring vacantly into the distance.